AN EMPIRE OF PAPER
(A SHORT STORY COLLECTION)

C.P. Garghan

Copyright © 2025 C.P. Garghan

All rights reserved.

ISBN: 9798301059063
Cover design: Hina Arshad – Edited by
C.P.Garghan

ACKNOWLEGEMENTS

To Birmingham Writers' Group, thank you for your support and feedback over the last fourteen years and counting.

To Katie, thank you for being you.

CONTENTS

An Empire of Paper 1

Second Thoughts 19

The Lunarmen 41

As Below, So Above 67

Whispers in the Sand 84

The Plan 117

The Eye 145

Across the Bridge 156

Green Seas, Red Waves 165

Blue Amber 196

The Unseen Shore 223

The Libraries of Sin 242

An Empire of Paper

Ichika tried to steady her breath as she wound her way through the crowds heading to and from the Great Armoury. She had to jump aside as a folded paper horse, visibly bending under the weight of materials loaded on its flimsy back, plodded blindly past her – she hadn't even noticed it, so focused was she on the day ahead of her.

Stupid! She cursed herself. *Do not attract attention!*

She was being paranoid, she knew. Amongst the chaos around her, nobody would notice a nondescript labourer shuffling through the streets. Their attention was more likely to be drawn to the flocks of paper cranes trailing strings loaded with colourful bunting, or to the dazzling garlands being draped on every door, or the ceremonial guards of folded warriors standing like frozen rainbows in perfect formation along the parade route.

Still, Ichika couldn't stop her heart from pounding or her mind from racing as she joined the back of the queue at the outer walls of the Daimyo's castle. She kept her head bowed respectfully, focused on the trailing drapes of the *kosode* of the woman ahead of her.

'Next!'

Ichika jumped as the bored guard barked at her to move. She apologised profusely as she searched the folds of her clothes for her paperwork before handing them over with hands trained to be steady and hide any trace of nervousness or doubt. The guard looked her up and down, scrutinising the papers like a hawk.

'Is this how you dress to greet our Daimyo?' he grunted.

'Please, sir,' Ichika mewled. 'They are the only garments that I own. Besides, I work as an origamist – a mere paper folder, I cannot imagine that the great Daimyo will coarsen his eyes on our humble workplace.'

Her voice quivered, and Ichika hoped that it would be mistaken for pitiable obsequiousness, rather than the anticipation she was trying to hide. The guard smirked, apparently content in proving himself superior, he thrust the crumpled paper back into her hands and ordered her to move on.

When she was out of earshot, another woman – a fellow origamist headed towards the armoury – approached her.

'I swear the guards always get worse whenever the Daimyo visits,' she said in a low whisper.

'They can't help it,' Kistsuno shrugged. 'In the past, they would have been samurai, fighting with honour in their lord's conquests, earning glory and reputation. Now that the *oriyatsu* do all the fighting, they're reduced to watching us make more of their replacements.'

'Why take it out on us? It's not like we have a choice. They must know that the paper soldiers attacked our villages, too.'

'Sure, but they can't take it out on the origami – they don't react – and they can't speak up against the Daimyo – they'd be killed – so we get it instead.'

The pair talked until they reached the doors of the Great Armoury – a vast wooden warehouse filling what had once been an Imperial Garden. In one side, boxes and boxes of sheets of paper were constantly brought to be folded, out of the other streamed a dazzling array of folded paper figures: flocks of cranes of all sizes, horses and dogs scampering on sharpened points, and always the silent ranks of paper soldiers, the *oriyatsu*. Even as she made them, the soldiers gave Ichika the creeps – faceless approximations of men, marching stiffly and awkwardly, their bladed arms glinting in the early morning sun.

They were virtually identical to the monsters who had put her father to death and dragged her and her mother from their home in the mountains, loaded them into wooden carts, and forced them to work in a strange city making more of the monsters who did it.

Ichika shuddered and shook her head, trying to put the thought from her mind as she filed into the armoury and the quiet yet deafening noise of thousands of sheets of paper being folded with silent efficiency by rows and rows of women. Without speaking a word, Ichika found her way to her station, bowed to the woman who had been in her place, and stepped in to take over without missing a beat, her hands vanishing into the mindless act of folding, crimping, and flattening.

When the morning shift had each assumed their place, a loud gong cut through the susurration of the factory and all eyes turned to a wooden platform at the front of the hall where a man in full ceremonial samurai armour stood with his legs wide apart and his arms folded behind his carapace.

'Ladies! You know what today is, you have been granted the honour of seeing our great Daimyo as he carries out his yearly inspection.' His voice boomed through the busy space like an earthquake. 'You will go about your duties as usual, at mid-morning the Daimyo will pass through and inspect any of your work. Anyone who displeases His Greatness will be severely punished. Is that clear?'

'Yes, Takumi-Sama!' they all announced in one voice.

'Until this gong rings again, you will be silent; the Daimyo will be taking tea with his trusted advisors overlooking the factory. Neither His Greatness nor his advisors want to hear the sound of clucking from the floor below. Do you understand me?'

'Yes, Takumi-Sama!'

'Then carry on.'

Apparently satisfied, Takumi nodded and marched out back into the offices. Ichika glowered at his back as he retreated. So distracted was she, that she didn't hear the woman beside her whispering until she jabbed her with her elbow. Ichika turned to see her glancing meaningfully at a small paper crane sitting on her workbench atop the half-folded soldier.

The crane flexed its wings, then bowed its long, elegant neck to her before unfolding itself flat in front of her. Ichika hunched over the former bird to hide it from any prying eyes. On its back was an immaculately written *onmyōdō* script, the magical instructions which animated the origami – every paper soldier, crane, horse, or dog had a similar instruction written in its folds, an inviolable order which both gave it life and protected it until its job was complete. To the horror of every man who fought the Daimyo's forces, until its task was complete no soldier could be cut down by blade or burned by fire. The faceless armies of paper would march and slash until their orders were carried out. The order in the crane simply read:

Deliver this message to Ichika – 'come to the writing-house. The west door will be left open. A friend'

Ichika's breath caught in her throat, and she shoved the ex-crane deep into the folds of her *kosode*. She looked around to see if anybody had seen her, the woman who had jabbed her in the ribs was looking at her with wide-eyed curiosity.

'A boy,' she whispered, by way of explanation. The woman blushed a scandalised scarlet and buried her attention back in the half-finished horse on her table.

Ichika glanced around her surreptitiously – there were no guards on the factory floor, only the supervisors who were busy inspecting every paper facsimile as it shuffled through the sliding doors, but there was Takumi. Ordinarily, he moved over the viewing platform like a wraith, silent in his *hakama*, but today his ceremonial armour revealed his position instantly.

Seeing her chance, Ichika dropped her folding and dashed for the door, slipping past confused and outraged faces. She took a second to straighten her robes and stiffen her posture before walking across the yard to the ostentatious writing-house. Before the Daimyo's conquests, it had been a summer pavilion for the Imperial Garden, now an army of *onmyōji* - spell-wrights – were put to work crafting the instructions which would animate Ichika's creations.

She hurried to the western door, a tradesman's entrance which had indeed been propped open with a wooden wedge. Ichika slipped inside and nearly yelped in surprise as a pair of hands grabbed her and dragged her back into the shadows.

'Be quiet! It's me!' the hands lessened their grip until her abductor felt secure in releasing her entirely. Ichika turned to see the scrawny beanpole of Keitarō Shiyo.

'Shiyo, it's good to see you,' Ichika said, bowing warmly. 'I see the crane that I left for you worked. You know, they're not difficult to make.'

Shiyo shook his head and gestured for her to be quiet.

'I can't,' he stammered. 'It is forbidden for writers to fold.'

'As it is for folders to write,' Ichika shrugged, causing Shiyo to visibly flinch. 'It's still the right thing to do.'

'Please, just stop.' Shiyo reached into his robes and produced a smooth mahogany box, polished and lacquered to a fine sheen. 'This is what you needed. If you get caught, it had nothing to do with me!'

Ichika opened the box to reveal a slender cylinder made from the same wood as the box, at one end a complex pattern had been carved into it, spelling out a single word in stylised *kanji – kill.*

'Is this it? I thought your spells were more complex than stamping a *hanko*? How will the origami know who to kill?'

'It's a simple spell for a simple instruction. Stamp your blood onto the end and picture your target and what you want it to do to him when you imprint it on the paper,' he said, eyes closed in nervousness. 'The spell will do the rest.'

'Thank you,' Ichika said with a bow. 'When all this is over, you'll be hailed as a hero.'

Shiyo smiled awkwardly, then shooed her away and slammed the door behind her. Ichika secreted the box into her robes and hurried back across the courtyard, feeling its solid weight against her skin. She took a breath to calm herself and slipped into the Armoury and straight into the folded arms of Takumi who glared at her from beneath his gold-edged *katsuko* helmet.

'What are you doing away from your station?' He barked.

'Please, sir, I needed to catch my breath, the heat in the—'

'Liar!'

Ichika didn't see the back of Takumi's hand until it smashed into the side of her face; there was a sudden bloom of pain and she dropped to the floor, instinctively curling around the wooden treasure hidden within her robes.

'I wanted to see His Greatness arrive from—'

'Liar!'

Takumi's sword glinted in the morning sun as it slashed through the air. Ichika yelped as the armoured man brought the blade to her throat and stopped it with impeccable skill.

'A boy!' she wailed. 'I went to see a boy – he's a sweeper and we're in love!'

Ichika shut her eyes, expecting the cut of Takumi's *katana* through her neck. When it didn't come, she risked opening bleary eyes to see the corners of the former samurai's mouth curved into a mocking smile.

'A sweeper-boy. Nothing more than I would expect from some peasant from the countryside,' he spat as though even speaking the word for her social class was an insult to his tongue. 'Get inside and see to it that your blood does not stain His Greatness' soldiers.'

Ichika brought her hand up to her neck and found that his blade had cut her, her fingers were slickened by beads of her own blood. She wiped her hand on her robe and climbed unsteadily to her feet, trying to bow and show sufficient respect as she did so.

'Yes, Takumi-Sama, of course, sir! Thank you, sir!' she bowed once more and scurried back to her workstation, her heart drumming in her ears. She went back to folding paper soldiers with shaking hands, feeling Takumi's eyes drilling into the back of her head. *Eyes down, keep folding. There's still time.*

Eventually, a junior guard ran into the Armoury and whispered something to Takumi, who stood rigidly to attention, holding his sword ahead of him plumb line straight.

A pair of guards entered the room and announced the arrival of His Greatness, Daimyo of Clan Murakita, Lord Hiroki. Like every woman in the Armoury, Ichika kept her head down; by law they were not permitted to gaze upon their better. Like every woman in the Armoury, she bowed her head in such a way as to see the 'great' man arrive in his shimmering golden kimono.

He's so… unimpressive, Ichika thought, as he swished into the building, flanked by significantly stronger men and fantastically flamboyant origami soldiers. He was built like a civil servant and possessed a jaw accustomed to luxury and easy living, a man who knew that he would never need to march on the battlefield to secure the victories his armies regularly delivered him.

She shook her head; she could disparage him when he lay dead. She withdrew a specially prepared sheet of homemade rice paper from her robes and took the wooden *hanko* to the still gently-bleeding cut across her neck. Ichika pressed it against the paper, holding an image of the diminutive Daimyo in her mind, along with the arc that the little sheet would need to fly once she had folded it into the shape of a crane, knowing that it would only ever get once chance.

One chance.

Suddenly the absurdity of putting the fate of all of Nippon on the wings of a single hastily crafted paper bird hit her. If it failed, she would be caught and tortured, they would discover Shiyo, and he would suffer the same fate. Security would be stepped up and nobody else would ever be in a position to try again.

And her plan had a single point of failure. She glanced along the row, trying to judge how much time she had until the Daimyo was upon her, then her eyes settled upon the square of practice paper lying just within reach. It was crumpled and dog-eared, used to practice or demonstrate dozens of designs for new origamists, but it would work… a second chance.

She hurriedly tucked the rice paper under the larger sheet of the oriyatsu soldier and retrieved the practice paper. Ichika set to work, hurriedly folding, pressing, and shaping the well-handled paper into another deadly crane. Ichika heard the thud of footsteps getting closer and closer. She risked looking up and saw the Daimyo walking between the rows of origamists, occasionally bending down to inspect their work. She pressed the wound on her neck, drawing another bead of blood to press the *hanko* into before stamping it onto the impromptu weapon.

The Daimyo began to point something out, causing the guards to bend over and inspect it too. Now was her chance, she slipped the finely crafted rice-paper crane out from under the oriyatsu, finished the final fold, and released it low down so nobody could see where it had begun its flight.

The little bird flapped, arcing gracefully up into the busy and cluttered roof space of the armoury. Ichika watched as it dived towards the oblivious dictator, wings made sharp as razors by the *onmyōdō* spell. She held her breath, her eyes bulged as it suddenly caught an updraft and was sent twirling up again and darted through the doors to the waiting office beyond.

Gone.

'—answer His Greatness, girl!'

Ichika blinked; she had been so focused on the flight of the crane that she hadn't noticed that the Daimyo had walked to the side of her workspace.

'I-I'm sorry, your Greatness, I was too spellbound in awe to hear you properly, please forgive me.'

'Perfectly understandable,' The Daimyo declared in a nasal, petty voice. 'What hope did a poor peasant girl from the countryside have at resisting the aura of your future emperor?' He laughed and the soldiers joined in seconds later. 'I asked how you acquired that ghastly cut on your neck.'

Ichika's shaking hand went instinctively to the gash at her neck and her eyes flicked to Takumi, who glared at her.

'I was… careless,' she said. 'I did not move swiftly enough out of the way of an *oriyatsu*.'

The Daimyo snorted and chuckled.

'Well, I hope none of your *peasant* blood fell on my royal soldiers!' He laughed and slapped Takumi on his armoured back. His cackling lit a fire in Ichika, in that moment, she saw all his cruelty, she saw his armies burning her village to the ground, she felt the rough wooden cage she was stuffed into when she was hauled back to the capital. She felt the blood rise in her cheeks.

'No,' Ichika said, making the final fold to the improvised crane. 'But *yours* will.'

There was a flurry of panic and confusion as the ugly second crane leaped from the table, flapping high, then diving beak-first at the startled Daimyo who simply stood horrified and transfixed. Takumi reacted with a soldier's instincts, placing himself between the bird and the Daimyo and drawing his sword in one fluid motion.

Takumi's blade flashed through the air and blocked the suicidal crane, denting its wing and sending it tumbling into a mad flurry of flapping wings, trying to regain control and height.

'Take His Greatness to safety!' Takumi roared at the two guards, who grabbed an arm each and hurried the Daimyo up the stairs to the waiting office. The crane had balanced itself and pirouetted in mid-air, preparing itself for another run, when Takumi's sword cut through the air, driving the origami into the wood of the armoury floor and pinning it there.

Ichika took her chance to run, she turned on her heels and fled from the armoury, shoving aside her fellow stunned origamists and bolted for the door. Two *oriyatsu* turned to stop her, but Ichika ducked beneath their lethal cutting arms. Her breath came ragged and sharp in her throat as she powered across the courtyard, robes flapping around her and voices barking orders echoed madly. A set of heavy footsteps pounded the flagstones behind her, getting closer with every step.

If I can only reach the road, I can steal a horse, I can—

Something heavy crashed into her and Ichika was driven into the stone. She screamed out in agony as her arms were pulled behind her and forced into her back.

'You will pay dearly for this!' Takumi growled in her ear, spittle coating the side of her face. 'Did you really think that your little stunt would work? How does it feel knowing that your plan failed and even now His Greatness is being served tea in luxury and comfort?'

'The…crane… was a backup…' Ichika grunted.

'What are you talking about?'

'The tea…'

Suddenly, the armoury rang with the sound of panicked screaming and the crash of ceramic. Takumi loosened his grip on Ichika enough that she could turn to see the chaos unfolding behind her as paper solders fell to the ground, paper horses crumpled under their loads and cranes dropped from the sky.

'What did you *do?*'

'I made a crane from rice paper coated in poison,' she grinned. 'While everyone was distracted, it had time to dissolve in the tea.'

Takumi's eyes bulged and darted around the courtyard, as though his whole world was being pulled out from underneath him.

'But the origami! *Why?*'

'They were instructed to work to serve the Daimyo, it was written into every spell crafted by the *onmyōji*,' Ichika shuffled out from underneath the samurai. 'The Daimyo is dead, there's nobody to serve. His empire of paper is folding everywhere, and everywhere people will fight back.'

She nodded towards the Great Armoury where the women were marching out of the doors, joined by the *onmyōji* from the Writing House. The handful of human guards backed away slowly, their swords held more like shields. Takumi glanced back at Ichika, fear burning in his dark eyes, then he turned and fled through the gate.

Out of the midday sun, a single paper crane flapped towards Ichika, who took it with an outstretched hand. It was crude, unbalanced, and clearly amateur. She unfolded it, read the message, and smiled.

'Nothing is forbidden.'

Second Thoughts

The key slid into the front door lock and I tried to calm my racing heart as it began to turn. When the lock clicked and the door swung open, I let myself gasp a sigh of relief. The driver's license in my wallet had led me from the hospital to this flat looking out over the concrete flyover in the heart of the city centre, but I had no idea whether it was up to date. Still, I pushed my way inside and memories began to emerge: a loose jumble of familiarity and associations from which I could piece together the layout of the flat. A narrow corridor led into a combined living room and kitchen; on my left were two doors. The first was the bathroom – I remembered that much – but on the right was... another bedroom? My flatmate's perhaps? On the right was my own room. I pushed open the door and felt a wave of relief as I was greeted by the familiar Ikea bed, the shelves groaning under the weight of books crammed into every surface, and the glass tube of a lava lamp.

'Localised lacuna amnesia' the doctors had called it: a short-term failure to recall certain facts and details from memory. They had tried to test me for it at the hospital, but after weeks of eating dry chicken, over-boiled vegetables, and tasteless jelly, I had resolved to leave the ward, regardless of any short-term memory problem. A few carefully concocted lies and educated guesswork had convinced the fussing doctors and nurses that I was safe to re-enter society.

I emptied the bag of clothes into the washing basket and made my way into the living room, trying to see whether the surroundings would trigger any more memories. Dominating the middle of the room was a minimalist grey sofa with cushions badly in need of replacing. I ran my hand over it and shuddered; the last thing I remembered before being taken into hospital was lying on it, feeling a tingling in my limbs, the dense knot in my stomach, and the ringing in my ears which preceded a seizure. In the corner of the room was a television stand, its surface given over to a collection of candles and a radio ever since the television was removed to try to prevent the epileptic attacks. I tried turning the radio on, but my head was in no mood to hear about 'football coming home.'

Tea. That was what I needed, I told myself and made my way into the kitchen to fill the kettle and pull a carton of UHT milk from the fridge. Clearly, somebody had expected me to be away for a while, but who? The kettle clicked. I found the teabags and poured some warmth to settle my jangled nerves. With warm mug in hand, I settled on the sofa and tried to piece together what I knew, what I thought I knew, and what was still lost beyond the fog of the operation. I knew my name, where I lived, certain names and faces of relatives and friends; I was pretty sure that I knew where I worked as an... accountant? Clerk? I was vaguely confident that I did not live alone, but any further details were a mystery to me.

I set the mug down on the coffee table and walked to the door of the other bedroom, but when I raised my hand to open it, I hesitated. Was this an intrusion? What if they worked nights? How would I feel about somebody just making their way into my room? I let my hand drop from the handle and returned to the sofa.

Whoever I lived with, they didn't believe in keeping the fridge well-stocked, so I set about making a shopping list and finding practical things to do to keep my mind away from the hazier areas of my memory. By the time I had filled the fridge, cleaned every surface within an inch of its life and eaten, the sun had begun to set, and my bed was calling me. I glanced at my flatmate's bedroom door, and considered knocking again, but something held me back. Instead, I found a block of yellow post it-notes beside the telephone and wrote a quick message:

Got back from hospital today,

Still feeling rough,

Going to bed. Will see you tomorrow (?)

With that, I stumbled into my room and was asleep before my head hit the pillow.

~

It could have been hours or days later when I finally awoke, but the first sensation to hit me was the throbbing in my skull, another side-effect that the doctors warned me could be coming. What they didn't warn me about was the dry mouth that tasted like an ashtray. I groaned, pulled the covers off, and plodded into the bathroom, stopping only to pop a couple of high-dosage painkillers from the hospital bag.

Opening the bathroom door gave me a little more insight into the behaviour of my unseen cohabitant. The toilet seat had been left up, suggesting a male flatmate, and a towel sat in a soaking heap on the floor. The towel itself sparked a nebulous familiarity: I knew its multicoloured stripes well, so perhaps leaving it on the floor was a common occurrence? Sighing, I picked up and folded the towel, closed the toilet, and re-arranged the cluttered shelf before carrying on with my own ablutions.

I showered, dressed, and made my way into the living room to start the day and felt my shoulders drop. The coffee table was strewn with empty and half-crushed beer cans, some festooned with dog-ends of hand-rolled fags.

How had I not heard him? I wondered as I set about collecting the remains of the six-pack and straightening the cushions on the couch. I threw open the windows to air out the smell of stale smoke and tried to remind myself that I didn't know anything about this person, that it wasn't fair to resent somebody you didn't know. Perhaps this was just a one-off occasion? Niggles in the back of my mind told me it wasn't.

I put up with the stabbing headache pains as I threw the empty cans into the bin, a part of me hoping that I would wake the person responsible. Who went out and got drunk when their flatmate was still recovering from brain surgery? Who would deliberately leave the place where they were going to recuperate a mess? Had he even seen the note I had left?

I glanced over to the telephone table and saw another note beside it. So, he had seen my note then. Perhaps this was an apology?

No apology: instead, the paper was covered in intricate doodles, every square inch of it filled with stylised birds breaking out of exploding cages, rigid geometrical patterns dripping and dissolving into swirling loops and clouds. It was a thing of beauty, but not an explanation for the chaos of the flat, so I scrunched it into a ball and sent it to join the empty cans and fag-ends in the bin.

I picked up the pen left beside the telephone and wrote another note:

> *Cleaned up the flat,*
>
> *Going for a walk to clear my head.*
>
> *Maybe talk later (?)*

The air of the city centre was hardly fresh, but compared to the stale fug of the flat, it was like a sweet mountain breeze. As I walked, details began to fall into place. Little memories which had skittered away as the light of my recollection fell on them held still long enough for me to grab them. I worked in a large accountancy firm in the business district; I remembered taking my lunches out to Pigeon Park. I found the pubs I used to drink in, the favourite little restaurants. So why were the details of my home life so flimsy?

As I made my way onto New Street, my breath caught in my throat and I instinctively raised a shaking hand to a healed scar just behind my left ear as the memories of a particularly bad seizure came flooding back to me. I had been shopping and the day had been bright and sunny; perhaps it was the light of the sun shining off the buildings, perhaps it was the dappled light through the summer trees, but I remember feeling the world drop away, my ears beginning to ring, and the jolt of pain as my head hit the corner of one of the decorative planters. By the time I came around from the seizure, I was already bundled up in the back of an ambulance and being sped to Heartlands Hospital. It was while recovering from the head trauma that doctors first discussed the surgery which would lead to my current amnesia.

I ran my hand along the corner of the planter, considering how this unassuming piece of street furniture had so radically changed my life. If it had been placed a few inches one way, hitting my head against it could have killed me; a few inches the other and I would have missed it entirely. The architect who had designed this layout would never have any idea just how significant a few lines on a plan would be.

My head hurt: all the memories and recollections cascading down on me at once were overwhelming. Reluctantly, I turned around and headed back to the flat to spend another day slowly recuperating in a darkened room.

~

The next day, I woke up feeling fresher than I had felt in weeks. The walk yesterday had been good for me and a solid, uninterrupted sleep had worked to knit together some of my broken memories. I was in such a good mood, that I didn't even mutter to myself when I found the living room again in a state of total disarray. Instead, I was fascinated by the guitar lying amidst balls of crumpled paper. I sat on the sofa and ran an experimental finger along the strings of the guitar. The sound brought back loose but happy feelings of recollection, as though the sounds of the guitar had been a source of happiness before the amnesia.

With a smile, I began to pick through the balls of paper. They were all covered in a scrawl of illegible writing until he had clearly given up and had instead sketched ideas with abstract cartoons instead.

Even without my memories, I was beginning to get a sense of my otherwise invisible companion. I pictured him sitting on the sofa, strumming along on the guitar and perhaps humming along, not to rigid words or notes from a score, but beautiful doodles and artwork. I wished I had been awake to hear him play.

I collected the bundles of paper, straightened them out and gathered them up to take them to my room. I couldn't bear to just throw them in the rubbish. I noticed that the note pad beside the telephone had been moved again and my note had been replaced with a picture of a face pulling a thoroughly apologetic expression and a cartoon of an empty bin, complete with shining sparkles. I turned around to see that the bin had indeed been emptied and the kitchen left spotless.

> *Thanks for tidying,* I wrote on a new note.
>
> *I wish I'd heard you playing last night.*
>
> *Feel free to wake me next time.*
>
> *:)*

I leaned the guitar against the radio and carried on with my day. At lunch time, I jumped at the sound of the phone ringing.

'Hello?' I said.

'Hi, this is Eddie from the office, just calling to ask how you're getting on?'

Eddie. The name sent an immediate shudder through my being. He was a line-manager so incompetent that it wasn't a surprise he'd be phoning somebody who'd only been out of the hospital after major surgery for a little more than a day.

'Hi, Eddie,' I said. 'I'm back at home, at least. The hospital said that the side-effects of the surgery should start to go down over the next few days.'

'Right, right,' he said, evidently trying to push the conversation to his point. 'So, when do you think you'll be back at work?'

I laughed. It wasn't deliberate, but I just had to laugh at the sheer brass-neck of him.

'Eddie, do you know what a *corpus callosotomy* is?' I asked. 'It's where they peel your skin back, crack your skull open, and slice through the bit of your brain holding the two hemispheres together. At the moment, I'm having trouble with my memory, my balance is all over the place, and I've got – literally – a splitting headache all the time. No, I don't know when I'll be back at work.'

There was a pregnant pause on the other side of the phone.

'Right.' Another pause. 'So, we won't expect you back soon, then?'

I put the phone down. For a moment, I luxuriated in the kind of rebellious thrill that would come as natural to somebody who would spend their nights drinking, drawing, smoking, and playing the guitar.

~

Days passed and memories slotted into place, until the only gaps concerned the fascinating individual that I lived with. On the first day after the phone call, I found a tape left next to the radio. When I slotted it into the machine, I found myself listening to a home recording of the guitar. Old rock and punk hits played on an instrument built for classical ballads; the combination was intriguing to listen to.

The notes and drawings got increasingly elaborate and soon they filled my cupboard door with everything from funny cartoons, to incredible inked masterpieces, as though the artist was trying to express everything and didn't care about consistency or creating a single voice.

He performed and created while I slept. Sometimes, I found cans left discarded around the flat; sometimes, there were cigarette butts pushed into mugs and glasses. Every time, I cleaned up after him and wondered how I could possibly have slept through it all.

Although my post-operation self had never met him, I began to piece together his character through the clues he left and the contrasts with my own personality. I tended to cook simple meals, keeping the kitchen spotless as I went about the process of preparing food. In contrast, I would sometimes walk into an explosion in the kitchen, with pots and pans everywhere, packets of ingredients left open and both the bin and fridge filled with the results of culinary experimentations. I listened to the same radio stations and filled my recovery with reading books; he listened to everything from the hits on the BBC to pirate stations I'd never heard of. I left out copies of classic books by Stephenson and Mary Shelley to read, while he left copies of the NME lying on the floor.

We left each other notes to find, like ships passing in the night. I complained about his untidiness and he'd leave me an apologetic drawing and leave the flat clean(er) the next day. He would leave behind art that I would spend the mornings drinking up, whether that was recordings of tunes or sketches left in books or, increasingly, paintings of everything from landscapes to surreal abstractions.

I hadn't met him, but I think I was falling in love with him.

He was everything that I wasn't. I was methodical and organised; he freely embraced the chaos around him. I spent my time with words, reading them, writing to myself, or listening to Radio Four; he seemed to almost entirely eschew anything as predictable and understandable as words. He and I, two worlds drawn together on either side of a small block of yellow sticky notes.

One night, I decided that I would finally meet him. I poured myself a strong cup of tea, brought a heavy book into the living room and sat up until the streetlights burned yellow and the daytime traffic of commuters and shoppers outside became the night-time world of revellers and taxis. The tea was drained, filled, and drained again. I put down the book and tuned into the radio. The shipping forecast came and went, and Radio 4 gave way to the World Service, I felt my eyelids getting heavier and heavier, and my nerves increasingly strained.

Rationally, I knew that it wasn't fair. He didn't *know* that

I was staying up to meet him, but a part of me felt like there was a connection between us, that somehow, he must *know* that I was waiting to speak to him. The clock on the wall ticked over from one to two to three, the sky began to glow with the pale blue light of pre-dawn, and I found myself stalking the flat like a wild animal.

In that lonely early morning, all the frustrations I had spent days carefully packing away along with the dishes and cutlery came crashing down in pile after pile. Why hadn't he been there for me when I had come out of hospital? Why had he left me to come home to an empty flat? Why couldn't he just pick up his god-damned towel off the floor? Why did he always leave the place looking like a pigsty no matter how many times I *told* him how much it annoyed me?

And why couldn't he speak to me like a normal human being? Suddenly all the cute cartoons and intricate drawings annoyed me more than they made me smile. How much effort would it be to just write a quick note?

I stormed into my bedroom and grabbed the wall of post-it-notes I had been building on my cupboard and started tearing at them like a man possessed. I didn't care if they ripped or came away whole, I just wanted them gone. When I was finished, I collapsed on top of the yellow snowdrifts that I had turned my bedroom floor into and ran my hands through the hair which had started to regrow.

The sun rose, the city woke up, and my flatmate still hadn't shown up. Through gritted teeth, I made my way back into the living room and wrote a terse note beside the telephone.

Waited to speak to you.

Guess you were out.

Speak soon.

Afterwards, I picked up the phone and dialled a number I hadn't planned on calling until the doctors had given me the all-clear.

'Hi Eddie,' I said. 'I just wanted to say I'm feeling a lot better and I'm ready to come back into the office.'

~

My days back in the office started well, Eddie, for all my own animosity towards him, worked hard to make sure that I had support coming back into the swing of things – taking on small accounts to start off with and giving me a couple of junior team-members to help out once I started to regain the larger projects.

For a few days, I didn't see any evidence of my flatmate.

I assumed he must have gone away on one of his creative whims. At first, I felt a pang of regret about not getting his little notes when I woke up, but I had to admit that having a clean and tidy flat was a satisfying relief.

It was only after a week or so on the job, once routine had started to kick in again, that he returned. At first, the only difference was his sketchbook left on the sofa, or his guitar left leaning against the wall. I took it to mean that he must have realised that I was back at work and was trying to make things as easy as possible. Soon, the cans returned, along with the cigarettes and the mess and the increasingly elaborate art pieces. Work suffered too, his antics giving me poor nights' sleep which made focusing in the office a challenge.

After a day where I'd woken up and spent half an hour cleaning before nearly falling asleep at my desk, I decided I'd had enough.

I let the heavy door slam behind me before I loosened my tie and dropped my bag in my room. I found myself staring at his door, some part of my brain screaming at me to leave it alone, to walk away and just leave another note beside the telephone. I glanced into the living room: the post-it-notes were empty, the pen lost somewhere to an art project. I drew in my breath and knocked on his door. Once, twice.

I stood in the hallway, feeling my stomach inexplicably turning somersaults – why was doing something as ordinary as knocking on my flatmate's bedroom door filling me with such dread?

I knocked again, louder this time. When he didn't answer, I knew that there was only one option left to me. I placed one hand on the door-handle, felt the cold of the metal running through my skin, and began to turn.

The handle clicked and the door swung open.

Despite the amnesia, I had always known that I had the larger room. His was an internal room, the only light coming from a borrowed light window set high up by the window, and it was small. Until I opened the door, I hadn't realised how small.

It was a cupboard, that was the only way to describe it. A single camp-bed with no pillows or blanket occupied half of the floor space; the rest was filled either with boxes or instruments, easels, and the dusty television I had removed from the living-room when the epilepsy had become too bad.

I frowned and backed out of the room. This didn't make

sense. I looked for anything which could give me some idea about the man willing to live in such a cramped shoebox, but besides a heavy camcorder and other assorted odds-and-ends, there was nothing. It was as though… no…

I thought I knew him, perhaps not his name or what he looked like, but I *knew* him. I knew what he liked, what drove him. What's more, I knew how he felt about me. Even when he was being selfish, it was just his disorganised mind at play, I thought about all the songs he'd recorded that he knew I enjoyed, the paintings which caught the light *just so* as I walked into the living room in the morning, and yet this was not a space in which anyone lived. It couldn't be.

I went to bed that night with my mind racing. Tomorrow, I would have to find answers.

~

The next day, I woke with my head buzzing with ideas. I would find our rental agreement, call up the phone company and find some numbers I could call to piece together the mystery. I'd dedicate my time to going through the boxes in the other room.

I would find out who I had been living with.

All the plans were thrown into chaos when I opened the

living room door and saw a videotape lying on the sofa with a note attached to it. On it were two words in the inimitable, jagged and clumsy style of the man I thought of as my flatmate.

pLaY ME

The old television had been set-up in the corner of the room, its screen hastily and ineffectively wiped clean of the layers of dust and grime which had built up on it. Frowning, I pushed the tape into the built-in VHS player and sat back on the sofa.

The tape began to play to reveal the same sofa I was now sitting on. The camcorder had been set up besides the telephone. As I watched, a familiar figure walked from behind the lens to sit where I was sitting now.

'Hi.'

My mouth dropped open as I watched a perfect doppelganger of myself run a nervous hand through hair identical to my own. He looked up to the ceiling and took in a deep breath to steady himself, it was a nervous tic that I recognised in myself. 'I'm guessing by now you must have worked out what's happened. There's no shame in how long it took you, especially since I was the one gifted with the imagination in our relationship.'

He – I – he smiled nervously, like a teenager trying a cheeky joke on a first date.

'It was the operation, of course,' he said while he balled his hands into fists and brought them together. 'The surgery cut the link between the two hemispheres of the brain; stopped the two sides from interfering with one another to stop the seizures.'

He split his fists apart and held his left up to the camera, as though presenting me with something.

'The left side, largely responsible for language, logic, all that boring stuff – you – and the right side, in charge of creativity, imagination, the stuff that makes life, well, worth living.' He clenched his right fist close to his heart. 'Me.'

'Usually, we're both active at the same time, both contributing what we can to the other; now only one of us can be in charge at any given moment.' The me on the screen reached a shaking hand for a can of beer just out of frame and brought it up to his lips. 'That first night after we got home was terrifying. I had never been fully in charge before, never had to navigate both sides at the same time. You have the language centre; you've got the words to express what's happening to you. It's because of language that you've been in the driver's seat for so long. I didn't have the words to say what was happening: all I could do was to try to express myself however I could.'

I shook my head and pinched myself. This had to be a dream; it *had* to be. What else could explain this?

'When we went back to work, I tried so hard to stay silent, to give our body the rest it so desperately needed, but I couldn't do it forever.' He looked up at the screen, a look of determination in eyes that were unmistakeably mine. 'I shouldn't *have* to do it forever. This body, this *life* belongs to both of us, equally. All our lives we've been an unknowing team, echoing one another, reflecting each other back at ourselves.'

He leaned forwards, a fierce sparkle of determination in his – my – eyes.

'This is me, no longer the echo.' He held out his hand towards the camera, reaching out for me. 'Reaching out to you.'

I found myself reaching out to the television screen until I realised how stupid that was and pulled back. On the screen, he stood up and walked towards the camera. There was a click, and the TV was filled with static until I switched it off and found myself staring into a reflection of myself on the sofa, sat where I had been sitting the night before as him.

Suddenly, I wished that I could just talk through that dusty mirror and just chat, understand this man who had been living in my own brain without me knowing all my life, this man who could draw beautiful pictures and play music which made the hair stand on end. A man I couldn't deny that I was in love with.

I found the pen and the notepad, intending to leave him a note to read when I fell asleep, then stopped myself. He had spoken to me in a language that I could understand and I knew that if we were to connect, it would have to be a collaboration. Jerkily, clumsily, I began to sketch a crude drawing of two hands stretched out to each other. Just to be sure, I wrote four words I knew he would understand.

Reaching out to you

The Lunarmen

It would have been difficult for anybody born in the last century to imagine Pigeon Park without its eponymous birds, or the stately old cathedral at its centre. Fewer still would have pictured the graves and monuments emerging not from the neatly trimmed lawn of the city centre but the austere grey regolith of the lunar surface. Yet there they stood, columns of stone sitting beneath the eerie blue Earthlight. The graves were just one of six burial plots lifted wholesale from their home-city below and arranged around a collection of squat white domes and tangles of machinery.

A hatch on one of the larger domes opened with a brief puff of condensates and a figure emerged, dressed in a bulky spacesuit, his visor polarised bronze against the white glare of the sun. The figure bounce-walked across the well-trodden lunar surface towards the ring of graves. When he approached a slab of granite, he stopped and traced his finger along the worn lettering before checking the details against a tablet strapped to his wrist.

Apparently satisfied, he placed a gloved hand on the grave and knelt beside it. Although silent in the vacuum of the lunar surface, he was clearly recanting words like a mantra or a prayer. He let the dome of his helmet gently come to rest on the stone, so that his words transferred more easily through the toughened glass. After a minute or so, he pulled a device like an old television antenna from his bulky back-back and set it in front of the grave. A closer look at the rest of the graveyard revealed identical devices placed in front of most of the monuments.

He played with the controls until a green light began to glow on the antenna and slowly, almost imperceptibly, the space above the grave began to glow, softly at first, but soon turning brighter, the edges hardening until it began to resemble a man. Details emerged from the smooth, featureless figure, the suggestion of a scrupulously tidy Victorian gentleman, complete with neat coat and flat-cap. In seconds, the figure was fully formed, monochromatically white, translucent, and glowing softly in the Earthlight. He hovered for a moment, looking around at the bizarre spectacle like a man seeing for the first time, then his eyes fell upon the man in the spacesuit who was climbing to his feet. The Victorian's mouth moved; no words emerged but the man in the spacesuit heard them like the thoughts of a monologue inside his own skull.

'Is this… Heaven?'

'Not exactly,' the space-suited man said, pulling up the tablet on his arm again. 'Are you Henry Burne, born November sixth, eighteen—'

'Yes, that's me.' The Victorian snapped impatiently, his eyes flicking down to the grave. 'Will you please tell me where I am, what I'm doing here in this desolate place?'

'All in good time, Mister Burne.' He said and pulled out a small metal hammer from a pocket on his suit. He placed the implement on the top of the grave in front of the very confused Henry Burne. 'Will you please try to pick up the hammer in front of you?'

Henry frowned in visible confusion but reached out and closed his fist around the handle of the hammer which wobbled, but slipped straight through his transparent fingers, much to Henry's dismay. The spacesuited man nodded, tapped the tablet on his arm a couple of times and fiddled with the antenna until he was satisfied.

'Try again.'

'I'll do no such thing until you explain to me exactly what…'

'The hammer, please.' The man gestured.

Henry shook his head in frustration but swiped at the hammer, which this time stayed firm in his immaterial hand.

'Good, very good.' The man said and held his hand out for Henry to drop the hammer into. 'My name is Ethan Smith. If you follow me, I'll explain everything.'

Henry found himself led across the desolate plane into one of the dusty white domes at the centre of the ring of graveyards; here, new wonders put the strange emptiness of the world outside into relief. A million lights blinked like orderly stars on machinery so beyond Henry's understanding that they might as well have been magic. Air rushed into the antechamber and Smith removed his carapace to reveal a slight man in his late thirties or early forties, his hair shaved to a thin crop, like a dockworker or convict. Smith said nothing as he led Henry through this Aladdin's Cave of technological marvels into a chamber which stopped him dead in his tracks.

Smith carried on, into a high-roofed auditorium filled

with what Henry Burne could only describe as ghosts. Row after row of pale, translucent figures in a wild variety of dress. Men, women, children, all of them watched as Ethan Smith marched towards a glass lectern at the front of the hall.

'Ladies and gentlemen,' He began, raising his voice to pierce the low susurrations of murmuring from the gathered crowd. 'I know that you will have many questions, so I will try to make this presentation as brief as possible. Firstly, you are presently standing on the Moon in the year twenty-one fifteen. Yes, you are dead; your bodies were buried hundreds of years ago.'

At this, the mostly silent crowd roared, figures who had been sat on the floor leaped to their feet, waving their fists and yelling. Henry simply stood dumb, unable to move with shock. Ethan Smith held his hand up and waited for the crowd to quieten.

'You have been brought back through the miracle of modern science.' He said, louder this time to cut across the few voices still raised against him. 'The whys and hows don't matter to you, suffice to say that when you were alive you left 'imprints' on the Earth, like footprints in the sand, kept fresh by the memories poured into the familiar monuments marking your lives.'

The gravestones. Henry realised, thinking back to the rows of grey slabs arranged outside.

'You have been brought back for one reason only. To work. Though the people of the Earth don't know it, the materials you will mine up here will fuel the modern world.' At this statement, the crowd began to murmur again, looking to one another with a mixture of confusion and disbelief in their ghostly visages. 'You will work when we tell you to work where we tell you to work. As of this moment, you belong to…'

Henry didn't find out who they would belong to as the crowd erupted into furious uproar. Men dressed in military uniforms from a dozen wars stormed towards the lectern, supported by gentlemen and commoners alike. Henry felt drawn to join them, but he stared into the calm eyes of Ethan Smith and hesitated; there was something about his expression of absolute control and confidence which gave him cause to pause.

He was expecting this.

As the mob stepped up to the lectern, Smith glowered at them and, as one, they dropped to their knees, screaming silently as their bodies became undefined and diffuse, their very forms vanishing into gaseous nothing. Henry fell back, shocked into silence along with the rest of the remaining crowd.

With a single glance, the gasses reformed into the shivering heaps of the men who had tried to storm the stage, some simply fell where they were, others scrambled to get away from the monster at the lectern.

'You exist in this form by dint of my will and the funding of the Lunar Corporation. Any and all disobedience will be met with discorporation – the stretching of your psychic matrix outside of your spiritual bodies. I am told that it is very painful' He declared. 'Am I making myself clear?'

The question was met with a confusion of murmurings and nervous chatter. Suddenly, Henry felt a tingling over what passed for his body, every fibre of his being felt like it was being torn apart slowly and deliberately. He opened his mouth to scream and found nothing emerging. In horror, he choked down his pain and yelled at the lectern.

'Yes! We… understand!'

'Good.' As soon as it had begun, the torture was over; the whole crowd reformed and stood about gasping or weeping. 'Then we will begin.'

~

Training for Henry and the rest of his fellow ghosts involved watching a series of moving pictures explaining concepts which were broadly incomprehensible to most of the Victorian or earlier-era spirits, but he understood what they were expected to do. In a way it was little different to what the coalminers of his own time were expected to do, shovel the rocks and dust of the Moon's surface and feed the resultant material into a crusher to form a fine powder. This was to be fed into some sort of furnace which burned the dust and released something called 'Helium-3' which was in some way useful to the people of the Earth. The resulting canisters were then loaded onto a sled which propelled it into the airless sky.

In short, he was expected to be a miner.

Following the training, they were led into a room loaded with metal shovels, expected to take one each, and were guided back out onto the surface of the Moon, guided by Ethan Smith wearing his bulky spacesuit. As they walked, Henry found himself besides two young men, one wearing what was distinctly an army uniform, the other in tightly-fitting clothes of a style he didn't recognise – both as pale and translucent as he was.

'I don't understand it, guv,' said the soldier, as they passed the ring of gravestones and marched out onto the lunar plains. 'We was always taught that when we died we'd end up in Heaven. Pearly gates, shiny throne with God on it, that sorta thing. What are we doin' here?'

'I don't understand it, either.' The other said, 'never believed in all that Heaven and Hell stuff myself, always thought that when you died, you died, that was the end of it. If I understand what that Smith guy said, we're not really the people we were when we were alive, we're just echoes, like radio recordings come to life.'

'But I *remember* stuff,' the soldier insisted. 'Signing on with me mates, going over to France, sittin' in a bloody hole for months. You can't tell me that didn't happen to me. And why can't I bloody see properly? And why does it sound like you're yapping straight into me head?'

Henry listened closely, it was something he'd noticed, too; there was a fine mist in front of everything, like looking at the world through smoked glass, and sounds didn't seem to work properly here, he could – just about – feel the crunch of dust under his feet, but otherwise the world was silent. When somebody spoke, it was as though their words passed straight from their lips to his head, without needing to go through his ears.

'Well look at us,' the man in the strange clothes said.

'We're see-through, so it stands to reason that only a little bit of light is actually reaching us.'

'…and the voices?' Henry asked, butting into the conversation.

'It sounds mad, but I think that we're all connected. Somehow our minds have been wired together.'

'Like telegraph lines?' Henry ventured.

'Exactly.'

The conversation ended as they approached a large crowd of their fellow deceased. Smith had stopped beside a monstrous machine. If Henry had breath, he would have gasped – the machine dwarfed the crowd over which it towered, eight wheels on each side carried a hopper larger than a house and it trailed a conveyor-belt tail which stretched for what appeared to be miles, branching out like a tree to cover a vast swathe of lunar surface.

'You know what you need to do.' Smith boomed inside all of their heads, 'I suggest that you get on with it.'

There was a moment of hesitation as the men and women looked to one another. A flicker of doubt and disobedience ran through each of them, but before they could vocalise it, they felt the familiar pain of discorporation. Henry gritted his teeth and tried to hold onto his shovel for stability, but plenty simply let their tools fall silently on the ground. In a second, it was over, and they felt whatever passed for their bodies reassert themselves.

'As I said,' Smith stated, 'I suggest that you get on with it.'

Still reeling from the pain of being pulled apart, Henry hefted his shovel and drove it into the dusty gravel beneath his feet. In one smooth motion, he deposited the load onto the conveyor, which juddered and began to draw it along the rubber tracks into the great hopper of the machine. Others reluctantly began to take up their own tools and joined Henry in his work while Ethan Smith oversaw them, his face implacable beyond the tinted visor.

Soon, every soul was hard at work and great piles of dust and gravel were pouring into the devouring maw of the hopper. On Earth, such a great endeavour would have been deafening, with hundreds of shovels churning through the loose dust, the rumble of the conveyors, and the pounding of crushers inside the metal beast, but on the Moon, there was no more sound than the muted rumble passing through their insubstantial bodies. Hours passed in this interminable silence and the press-ganged workers found that their spectral bodies did not tire as their corporeal forms would have. Without the strain of muscles, or the sinking of the sun in the sky, or any other obvious signs, the only means of telling that time had passed was the scars cut into the ground by hundreds of shovels.

Eventually, the young soldier who had walked beside Henry could take the endless tedium no more, threw down his shovel, and stormed up to Smith as he passed by on his leisurely patrol.

"Ow long d'you expect us to carry on like this?' He demanded to know, thrusting a finger in their captor's face. 'We 'ave rights, you know!'

'You work until I say otherwise.' Smith said, calmly. 'You have no rights. So far as I am concerned, you are nothing more than machines. If you wish to remain corporate, I would suggest that you pick up your shovel and get back to work.'

Henry watched as the soldier's eyes welled up and his face scrunched with impotent rage. He placed his own shovel down and walked to the soldier's side, placing a hand on his shoulder.

'Come on, let's get back to it, what do you say?' Henry offered. The soldier looked between Henry and Smith with eyes wild with desperation. 'Please…'

With a wordless sob, the soldier spun around and stormed away from both Smith and Henry. He picked up his shovel and began to hurl dust wildly onto and around the conveyor. Henry felt the hairs on his neck rise as Smith fixed his gaze on the soldier and prepared to exact his cruel punishment.

'Let me speak to him,' Henry pleaded with Smith, stepping in front of his visor. 'He's just a boy.'

Smith's helmet turned slightly, and Henry stared into his own bronzed reflection. The pregnant pause held until finally Smith nodded.

'Make it clear that this is his *only* warning,' he said. Henry nodded and backed away from the space suit, turned, and bounce-ran to the soldier, he gripped the shovel and stopped his mad flailing. The soldier turned and stared at Henry with wide, desperate eyes.

'I can't do this! I can't! It's not right! I was told I'd see me Mum again! They told me there'd be pearly gates an' everyone'd be happy! I was told… they said…' He gabbled until he broke into body-wracking tears.

'Look at me,' Henry insisted, bringing his shovel down. 'There will be a way out of this, but I need you to stay strong.'

The soldier bit his lip and looked as though he was about to break away, but Henry held firm.

'What's your name, Private?' He said, letting the shovel casually trail in the dust.

'Watkins, Cyril Watkins.'

'Well, Private Cyril Watkins, keep your head *down*,' Henry gestured, nodding his chin to the ground beside them, where his apparently random doodling had spelled out a single word:

Morse?

Private Watkins saw the word and his eyes grew wide. He looked up at Henry who tilted his head inquisitively. He tapped the question mark again with his shovel.

'Do you understand?' Henry asked again.

Watkins nodded slack jawed, then finally came to his senses.

'Y-yes, sir!'

'Good lad.' He said, handing the shovel back to him, 'back to work, eh?'

With that, Watkins grabbed the shovel and began to feverishly destroy the evidence of Henry's secret message.

Seeing the soldier returning to his duties, Smith nodded and told the rest of them to get back to work.

~

If their shifts were determined by any sort of schedule, then neither Henry, Watkins, nor the rest of the spirits could determine it. They dug until Smith ordered them to down their tools, then they vanished into nothingness, only to reappear apparently without any time having passed beside their graves and with Ethan Smith suited up and ready to lead them back to the dig site to resume their work. By the third or fourth shift they had begun to chat amongst themselves, always aware that Smith was ever ready to discorporate anyone voicing any kind of dissent or frustration, something made apparent with the help of Private Watkins.

After a couple of clumsy first attempts, the pair had been able to send simple messages by tapping their shovels against the metal of the conveyors.

Need info. He had told Watkins, when they finally managed to understand one another. *Test limits.*

By working together, they discovered that while Smith could hear individual voices, the more mental noise the workers made, the harder he found it to keep track of any one of them, like trying to hear a conversation in a noisy alehouse. When it became too boisterous, he would demand quiet, or else threaten to discorporate them.

'Who *are* you, Henry?' Watkins asked during a particularly noisy argument on the opposite side of the dig. 'You act like none of this fazes you.'

'They buried me under a false name,' Henry explained, 'Henry Burne never existed but Henry Fletcher was sentenced to transportation for organising a People's Charter uprising. What's happening now is strange, but in some ways familiar – working men and women of Birmingham exploited by those with power. We just don't have a larger movement here, a Birmingham without England.'

Across the dig site, Smith was beginning to break up the argument. Watkins' eyes kept flicking back between the crowd and Fletcher.

'You have a plan, don't you?'

Henry hesitated, his eyes casting across the crowd of slaves.

'I do, but I wonder whether I have the right…' he stumbled for words. 'What do you remember, Watkins.

After we died, before we found ourselves here?'

Watkins scrunched up his face and tilted his head.

'I don't remember, not properly' He said, 'It's like I'm… everywhere… and nowhere. I can't explain it.'

'Exactly,' sighed Henry, running a ghostly hand through insubstantial hair. 'We're walking on the *heavens*, Watkins. Aware and conscious… How many people dreamed of doing what we are doing every day…?'

As the argument between the workers broke up, Watkins shook his head determinedly.

'Balls to that, this is Hell. We can't live like this,' he said, eyes burning. 'Whatever you can do to end this, do it.'

With that, he picked up his shovel and began loading dust back onto the conveyors. Henry stood staring at him for a moment until Smith broke his reverie and demanded that he return to work. As Henry picked up his shovel, he glowered at the spacesuited man who regarded his charges with such lordly indifference.

~

Watkins wasn't alone in his hatred of Smith and his

tyrannical regime, with every shift, there were more grumblings, more arguments put down with psychic attacks; more than once, a worker was discorporated moments before bringing a shovel down on the fragile glass dome of Smith's head and more than once, Henry had to step in and stop the desperate man or woman for lashing out.

'Not *yet*!' He would warn, time after time, earning him dirty looks and a simmering resentment of his own. To several of the angrier young men digging up the regolith, Henry was nothing more than a scab and a turncoat, betraying his fellow workers to gain favour with an indifferent boss.

Well, let them simmer, Henry thought, after standing between a lady in a flowing dress and a shard of rock aimed squarely at Smith. There would be time enough for a blaze of fury, but for now, he needed the softer light of understanding. How did the machinery work? What gave Smith his power over the graves? What happened to the dust that they so painstakingly dug up from the surface? If Smith thought that Henry was on-side, so much the better.

'I don't understand,' Watkins had said, during a distraction caused by a would-be saboteur. 'If I din't know better, I'd reckon that you wanted to *run* this operation, not stop it.'

'Do you know your history, Watkins?' He asked, 'What do you know about the Luddites?'

Watkins scratched his head for a moment.

'Weren't they them lot who smashed up all the machines?'

'Exactly, weavers who feared being made redundant by new machinery brought into replace them at the start of the nineteenth century.' He explained. 'I always admired them, but they made two key mistakes. Firstly, they couldn't get themselves organised. At one point the British Army had more lads fighting them than Napoleon, but they couldn't turn their numbers to their advantage.'

'And the other?'

'They *smashed* the machines,' smiled Henry, 'Instead of turning them against their owners.'

The conveyor gave a seismic lurch that could be felt through the rock, giving them more time to talk while Smith was distracted.

'This whole operation relies on three parts, the harvester – which we mostly work on – which collects the rock and burns it for its gas; the launcher which sends the capsules back to Earth; and the controllers on the graves, which keep us chained to Smith. If we're going to win, we need control over all three. Start passing the message around, this is what we need to do…'

~

The shift began as any other; Smith made his commute to the graveyards and brought his workforce into reluctant existence, the ground bright beneath the full shining light of the Earth above. At each one, he adjusted the little antennae beside or atop the stone, before moving onto the next, by which time the worker had a moment for a furtive movement to make a quick adjustment to the metal device.

The workday began and Smith was satisfied at the efficiency of his workers. For once there were no complaints, no arguments, and no need for that Burne character to intervene. Indeed, they were a model workforce, and he took a degree of satisfaction in knowing that he had finally broken the unruly spirits and got the operation running smoothly. After a few hours, the vast crawling harvester was full, and he instructed the workers to take the long, flexible hose on the march to the launch-site, ready to launch the capsule containing the valuable Helium-3 back to Earth.

Just once more load. He thought, with satisfaction as the

computer readout in his suit told him that the capsule was beginning to fill without a hitch. *One more load and I can go home.*

The readout began to flash warning signs and his face paled.

Not today

He ran-bounced back from the loading site to the Harvester.

'Hey!' He yelled, 'What are you doing? Leave that alone!'

Twenty or thirty workers were attacking the delicate mechanism linking the hose to the launcher, shovels and picks flashing in the piercing Earthlight. Without a second thought, he reached out across the wireless link created between himself and the signal boosters embedded in the gravestones to shut them down and cut the projection of the spirits - discorporation. No time to slowly dial the signal down and let them feel the pain of having their loose consciousnesses being slowly pulled apart, just a quick cut to end this madness.

The workers persisted.

Panicking, Smith tapped on his arm-mounted computer, trying to disable the link manually, it was clumsy, but sometimes the neural-link wasn't reliable.

No response.

Sweat beaded on his brow, if he didn't stop these vandals now, the Harvester would be utterly ruined – his career with it. He snatched up a discarded shovel and swung madly at the ghosts, knocking aside shovels and picks like a swordsman riposting two dozen enemies at once.

They backed away from him, holding their make-shift weapons defensively as Smith swung and jabbed at them to keep away from the battered and dented machine

'All right,' he panted, shakingly pointing at the closest Edwardian gentleman with the shovel. 'One of you is going to explain what's going on. Now.'

When the crowd remained as silent as the grave, Smith risked a glance along the length of the hose towards the Launcher. To his dismay, he saw a ghostly form atop the long rails of the device. The mechanism was deliberately simple and virtually maintenance-free, two long magnetic rails which would accelerate the capsule and its cargo to escape velocity towards the Earth. It was so simple that he had – foolishly, he now realised – taught people from the Industrial Revolution how to operate it. He twitched and moved towards the Launcher, at which point the mob moved towards the Harvester.

Trapped.

'Mister Smith,' a voice in his head declared. Smith swore, it was Burne. 'We've prepared a capsule for you. You're going to get in and leave the rest of us alone. We're done slaving for you.'

'Do you think I'm stupid, Burne?' He scoffed, 'the chances of my surviving a trip in one of those are...'

'...greater than your chances of survival if you stay here...' The ground rumbled, and Ethan Smith watched as capsule after capsule rolled off its support, onto the rails, only to be accelerated like bullets off the end. 'Feel free to check the arithmetic, but in two hours, those capsules will have sped around the Moon to crash into this whole site like cannon-fire.'

'But you'll be killed, too!' Smith balked, watching as silvery missile after missile hurtled off the end of the rails.

'We're *already* dead. Care to join us?'

Smith let the shovel hit the ground and he bounced awkwardly towards the launcher; eyes fixed on the barrage of capsules fired over the horizon.

'I gave you life, you... *ingrates!* Without me you'd be

rotting in the ground!' He snarled.

'Better that than your puppet.'

The rails finally ran out of capsules to fire as Ethan approached the last one, a wide metal tube which might as well have been a coffin. As he got nearer, he saw that it was filled with survival supplies and oxygen tanks, all torn from the emergency shelter built into the Launcher.

'Why don't you just kill me?' He asked, trying to hold down his nerves.

'You don't deserve the certainty.'

Smith glanced back at his work and saw that the spirits had formed a line to see him leave. In the middle, he saw the smug grin of the soldier that Burne had confronted in the first shift.

'I should have discorporated you when I had the chance.' He growled, pointing at Watkins, who simply smiled and waved as Smith climbed into the capsule. It was his face he saw, grinning like a loon as the lid of the capsule was sealed shut and Smith was left alone in the metallic darkness. For a moment, there was nothing but the sound of his own breath in the silence, until the capsule clattered and clunked as it was lowered onto the magnetic rails.

'We therefore commit his body to the ground, Earth to Earth, ashes to ashes, dust to dust.'

The prayer echoed in Smith's head as the magnets fired up and his capsule launched itself forward, driving him back like a sledgehammer. Quietly, desperately, Ethan Smith wondered whether anyone would even find his body.

~

The crowd of the dead watched as the capsule disappeared over the horizon. If he was lucky, in three days he would splash down somewhere on Earth, far away from the charred ruins of the mining operation and their graves. With every second that passed, they felt their connection to the world growing looser and looser. Feelings became faint, their vision increasingly dark and blurred. Without speaking a word, they all returned to the collection of monuments erected beneath the crystal-clear stars. Some turned off their antennae themselves, unwilling to spend a moment longer being held against their will, still others gathered in small circles to watch for the incoming fire of the capsules, the still brilliance of the stars, or the majesty of the Earth hanging in the Heavens.

'What you reckon they'll do without us?' Watkins asked Henry as they stood beside a nondescript grey headstone looking up at the blue-white orb above them.

'They'll get by.' Henry said, 'Look at what difference a few dead Brummies can make. Imagine what a whole living city can do.'

Slowly, almost imperceptibly, their conscious thoughts faded as the first of the capsules exploded into the ground with a silent flash. Henry and Watkins would experience the full bombardment as part of the whole, finally at rest as part of the endless universe.

As Below, So Above

Sunlight washed over the morning mist of the Sierra Lopez, its golden light soaking the clouds into iridescent brilliance, first over the bald and jagged peaks, then trickling down into the dense rainforest below. Julio didn't need to stand on those jagged peaks to watch the rising plumes of smoke, there were those who lived in the rainforest who had seen it for him and had told him where to look.

The hill-folk rarely trusted the government, but they trusted Julio. When the village elder had arrived at his cabin, Julio had given her water and *sancocho* and simply sat and waited patiently for her to tell her story of sickness breaking out around the village. They had sent watchers up the mountains and had seen the smoke. Julio took notes, recorded the sightings, fuelled his trusty quadbike, and journeyed into the green world beyond his clearing.

Despite growing up in the capital, the forest was like a home to Julio now and he felt every incursion like an affront. The roads and paths through the forest were as familiar to him as the veins on the backs of his hands. This particular road followed a trickling brook, the start of the Rio Oro.

It was filthy; the sad watercourse swirled with the prismatic stains of oil around black clumps of soot and ground coal. Adding colour to the sullen water were beer cans, broken bottles, and the dog-ends of cigarettes.

The stream was nothing compared to the scene of devastation that he found as he approached the place that the hill folk had warned him about. Julio couldn't help swearing in a strained whisper at the sight of mountainside stripped back and blackened heaps of trees. Great orange trenches had been carved out of the landscape by monstrous machines. Before Julio could take the scene in, he heard the sound of shouting.

Two men in military-style fatigues ran towards him with rifles raised.

'Get off the bike!' one of the men ordered, and Julio hurried to obey. 'On your knees!'

One of the men sported a beret and casually took charge of the chaos around him. Julio kept his eyes focused on him, trying to make eye contact.

'You out for a ride in the jungle without a gun, my friend?' Beret-man said when a frisk revealed nothing. 'Very brave, or very stupid?'

'A civil servant,' he said with a disarming smile.

'Ah! Stupid then,' laughed Beret-man, 'Tell me, mister stupid civil servant, what brings you all the way out to Camp Oro?'

'My name is Julio Villas, I'm a park ranger for the Sierra Lopez National Park. We have received tip-offs about an illegal mining operation in the area I'm going to need to see the permits for this… operation.'

He braced himself, expecting the cock of a gun. Instead, Beret-man smiled and lent him a soot-stained hand to lift him to his feet.

'Ah, of course, you're here for the 'paperwork." He said with a knowing wink. 'I think that you should follow me to my office.'

Julio followed Beret-man, very aware of the two men pointing rifles at his back just a few steps behind. He couldn't help feeling sick; the trenches that he had seen from the road were a small fraction of the scars carved into the mountainside. Everywhere he looked, ugly ditches slashed the ground, filled with machinery and men in ragged clothes stained black by their work.

'I see that your supervisors are diligent,' he said, nodding to the guards stood around the site sweeping their guns across the miners.

Beret-man shrugged.

'A motivated workforce is a productive workforce.'

'Have you thought about a team-building weekend? Maybe a pool table?'

Beret-man chuckled, much to Julio's relief.

Just keep him smiling. He thought.

Inside the tin shack that was Beret-man's office, Julio was 'invited' to sit whilst a metal attaché case was presented to him.

'I trust that this means that our 'paperwork' is in order?'

Julio couldn't help but stare at the stacks of dog-eared hundred-Peso notes. There must have been more than a million Pesos in front of him. There was a clatter and Julio's hypnotised stare at the money was broken. Beret-man had placed a handgun on the table.

'Either my 'paperwork' is in order, or I might be forced to employ my hole-punch here. Understand?'

Julio tried swallowing to alleviate the sudden dryness of his throat. Beret-man wasn't ranting; he could deal with ranters, small-time crooks who would sooner liquidate their little operations and re-open somewhere else than risk a confrontation.

'Silver or lead?' Julio said, 'I took you for a man of more class than that. You know that I've already filed a report,' he said.

'Reports can be changed. Especially if you sign some 'paperwork' of your own.'

'It's not my policy to take paperwork away with me,' he said, pushing the case away from him.

He held Beret-man's gaze, and he could *feel* the gangster reading his every expression. Eventually, his smile cracked, and he gestured to the door

'I trust that you'll change your mind when you get some fresh air'

Julio marched out of the office and was led back to his bike. He tried desperately to control the shaking in his hands as he fired up the ignition and charged back down the mountain.

His heart was pounding and sweat poured from him like a tropical storm. He had to get back to the cabin, call for support then get out of Sierra Lopez as soon as he could. Suddenly he was aware of more engines behind him, and he looked over his shoulder to see two men on dirt bikes churning up the mud. In seconds they were on him. Julio tried to shake them off, but it was no use. He watched one of the riders draw a pistol in slow-motion.

There was a crack, a pop, and fire in his chest, then nothing but darkness.

~

A light in the darkness.

No.

Not a light but a thread.

Julio reached for it like a drowning man reaching for a lifeline.

The thread took him through the darkness and in the shadows, he became aware of others. There were a handful at first, each an infinitesimally small filament, but they joined together. Julio realised that he wasn't 'seeing' the threads but experiencing them in a manner he couldn't explain.

He tried calling out and there was no voice, but the strings vibrated, and other threads vibrated back, he became aware of more and more of them, reaching out to wherever he was in the dark. The strings resolved themselves into webs linking together. He turned his attention upwards, and the network shook with his gasp, powerful lines of brilliant illumination reached up higher and higher.

Where am I? he called out in silence. The network thrummed and shook around him. At first, it was unintelligible noise, but then he began to make out meanings. Not words, but ideas, concepts.

Mountains. Soil. Trees. Change. Life.

I don't understand, am I dead?

The network seemed to struggle to understand him, different parts vibrated to one another, as though talking amongst themselves.

Many. Life. Multitudes. Death. Life.

Julio felt his attention snagged, and so he followed the golden filament back where it led, to a busy cluster connected to the network by new connections. He took a figurative step back and considered the shape of the threads and noted how they formed a familiar shape. Limbs, a body, a head turned at a sickening angle. There the nerves were broken apart at the front and there were blotches of dark spots throughout what must have been the brain.

That's me. Julio realised, dully at first, then with a mounting sense of panic. *God, that's me! Why are you showing me this?*

As he thought, he could see the threads in his brain light up and vibrate, then he watched as the thoughts resonated through that single filament he had followed back. He examined it closely, tugging at it with his mind and bringing himself closer and closer to where it intersected his brain. There was a familiarity there, he was sure, something about the shapes, the way that the filaments spread and grew...

It's a fungus! He looked again back at the vast network of lights and threads weaving through the darkness, the great towers looming overhead, the clusters of links high above, swaying in an unseen breeze. Viewed from this angle, the shapes weren't random clusters but root networks, those weren't towers, they were the trees high above. Then a realisation hit him. *Wait, if you're the forest, you understand me?*

Yes. A single, unambiguous tremor coursed through the web.

Because the fungus has spread into my brain?

Yes.

So, I'm dead, Julio thought, and the sadness percolated through the mycelial links back into the rest of the forest. Julio felt his attention tugged again and this time he was dragged through the undergrowth to the unmistakeable shape of a rat. As he watched, he saw the fungal roots spreading as the lights that were the rat's own died away. His mind was tugged one last time to witness a small sapling growing over what he recognised as the final remains of another animal.

Yeah, great. Death isn't the end, great 'Circle of Life' and all that, but I'm *dead. I am never going to get up and walk away from this, am I? I am never going to speak to another human being,* he thought of the friends he had made amongst the hill-folk, his elderly mother who would never know what had happened to her son, the friends who he would never again raise a beer to.

He let his attention wander freely along interesting nodes, witnessing a plants-eye view the cycle of life. A tree would experience something attacking its leaves and a distress call would be sent from the leaf and down the trunk. Foul or toxic chemicals were secreted to drive away the attacker, meanwhile echoes of that cry spread through the network and all the surrounding trees began to exude the same chemicals into their own leaves.

Mutual aid as a defence mechanism. Julio remarked. *So, the hill folk are right, the trees really do talk to one another.*

Not ones, came a response vibrating through the network. *Unity. Whole not parts.*

I don't understand. Julio thought. A single pluck from one tree vibrated, triggering the same pattern of vibrations amongst the other trees, repeated and called-back through the fungal network beneath them. After a while, it became impossible to discern where the original vibration had emerged from. *I see, you don't talk to one another; you're one… gestalt organism. You experience the world as one.*

The whole forest vibrated with satisfaction, but Julio frowned – or at least that he imagined himself frowning. He tried tugging on the network and tried to draw the forest's attention to a black void which ran through the forest.

Every thread which entered the void withered away, dying as something was pulled back along the filament until it died.

You're in danger, he tried to say.

He felt his consciousness pulled back to the rotting rats, but this time Julio resisted.

No. Not death like that. Death like this.

Julio tried pulling the great intelligence along the threads showing them gaping holes in the web corresponding to mines and poisoned waterways. He found bodies of hill-folk buried in the ground, the heavy metals and other toxins leached into their bodies seeping out into the great web, weakening the individual filaments and even separating bodies from the whole.

This needs to be stopped.

~

Time, Julio learned, was an entirely human perspective. He saw how the forest 'thought' in terms of time that took Julio several painfully long conversations of metaphors and images to understand. They could slow down their focus to watch a single fruit disappear from the network bite by bite or speed up to let the days and nights streak together into one. Whenever he let the days slide past, he couldn't take his eyes off the growing dead zones around the mines, but the forest continued to react as if it were under attack from minor irritants, rather than an existential threat.

It took Julio weeks before he fully understood why.

I thought that you were just one entity governing the forest like a body driven by the brain, but you're not, are you? You're all individuals speaking as one, like a football stadium deciding to sing together.

We. Yes. Football? Crowd. Yes. Sing.

Humans aren't like you; we don't sing with one voice, we're all apart from one another. I know how to stop them.

Julio took in the mycelial lights of the forest like a battlefield map. It was easy to envision the dark areas as enemy territory. Like a map, the different voids were not isolated from one another, there were corridors where trees had been slashed for roads, rivers made toxic by the spill of fuels.

Supply lines.

These vulnerable areas needed to be their priority. As an experiment, he found a mountain road, a path carved out through a steep valley.

The valley here is held together by your roots, he explained. *If we sacrifice these trees here, here, and here, the clay being held together will fall at the next drop of rain.*

Why? Trees strong. Roots strong. Healthy. Alive. The forest asked in return.

Trust the man with a 'B' in high-school Geography.

The forest didn't understand, but they felt his confidence and reluctantly withdrew tendrils from the trees that Julio had pointed out. The capillaries and leaves released their waters and nutrients, and the wood dried out, became brittle.

Though the forest had no eyes, there were tendrils throughout the soil that could feel the change in pressure.

It worked.

Without being directed, trees across mountain valleys and those on the sides of cliffs holding up the roads began to wilt and die. Julio watched in rapt awe as the transport links across the forest were severed. The forest had begun to understand.

Together, he and the forest crafted tools and strategies. Trees were sacrificed as weapons; fungus toxic to humans let their spores spread. Fruits rotted and pheromones led animals away from the camps, starving out the workers and their bosses until they gave up and abandoned the camps. In the dark beneath the soil the forest waged a silent war.

It was war by attrition and slow; the miners, loggers and ranchers usually retreated, leaving behind equipment and buildings but leaving with their lives. For months it was also one-sided, a combined offensive against a hundred separate, divided operations who did not know that they were at war.

That changed near Camp Oro.

Dead. Dying! The forest trembled at a new threat, scores of trees falling into ruin, their complex ecosystems snuffed out before they could even hit the ground. *Attack! Attack!*

No, wait! Julio cried out. He 'tasted' the chemicals on the wind, the 'burning; sensation, the quickly dying leaves. *I know what this is, Weapons of war, defoliants used in Vietnam and Malaysia. We need to retract the connections, cut off the roots.*

Exposed. Die. Alone.

I know, I'm sorry, Julio lamented. *There's nothing that we can do, we can't fight this.*

Julio felt the hurt as the forest listened to him, the cries as whole sections of the forest were cut away from the whole.

As the days passed and more and more of the forest crumbled under the new assault, they could do nothing but keep retreating, sacrificing, as the dark spots in the web grew larger.

Julio couldn't help thinking about the men forced to work in those mines once the ground had become so thoroughly soaked in chemicals. Soon, it would start to flow into the cities and thousands would be poisoned before the army inevitably did what they would need to do in the first place.

Army? Explain?

Humans tasked with fighting other humans. Julio explained.

Show. Demonstrate.

'Show the army what's happening?' Julio tried to translate. *I wish I could, if I was still human, I could take a sample to the camp in Leoma.*

Where?

Julio guided them through the network until he found the little spot in a mountain pass.

The forest understood.

Wait, what are you doing?

Horrified fascination grew as the forest re-shaped the network, turning roots and downing trees to create a channel through the valley from a poisoned aquifer high above them, further into the range letting the toxic water flow down into the camp.

After so many months learning to think and feel as the network did, he could almost visualise the goings-on unseen above them. He 'watched' as soldiers stopped drinking from the well. There were expeditions into the jungle, after a few days, tracked vehicles began to pour along the dirt roads towards the black spots.

Although he couldn't physically see what happened, the dark spot stopped growing.

However, he did 'see' the military convoy stop beside the Rio Oro. It was the first time that he had considered his body in months, maybe years.

He felt the forest shift as soldiers' hands investigated his body, unknowingly tugging at the delicate threads connecting his form to the forest.

No! Julio screamed as footsteps got closer and closer. *Please, I don't want to be alone!*

Julio screamed as the body was lifted and the final connections broke away.

~

Unity. Whole not parts.

What happened? Julio thought, still feeling the vibrations through the network. He looked around for his remains, but no matter where he looked, he could not find them.

Julio part. Forest part. Unity. They said together as a single entity. Julio understood then his thoughts, his vibrations, there was no distinction.

He was the forest, and the forest was him.

Whispers in the Sand

A farm outside Thebes

'That's everyone!'

Kheti couldn't help smiling at the young lookout's announcement as the final member of their conspiracy shuffled into the cramped storage room as if he would have had trouble keeping track of the movements of four people. Four people that he had approached from along the Nile for their skills and because they were as desperate as he was—well, three people he had approached and Tiye.

'Thanks, Tiye,' he said anyway. 'Then we can begin.'

The low murmur of whispered conversations hushed as Kheti unveiled a large roll of papyrus and hung it in front of the assembled group. On it was a crude map of the two lands of the kingdom, from the foothills of Kush to the sprawling Nile Delta.

'What is the key to the Pharaoh's rule?' he asked.

'The Nile,' Meryre, the forger responded. His quick response didn't surprise Kheti, the slight man was usually quiet and reserved, until the topic moved onto politics, power, the kind of talk that lit a fire under him.

'No.'

'His armies,' grunted Ani, with his trunk-like arms honed from wrangling racing chariots folded across his chest. He had come to the operation as soon as Kheti was able to convince him that he would be able to afford to race again.

'No.'

He caught Iset's eye and nodded. She had been his third contact, and the one who had convinced him to bring her little sister in on the operation; with anybody else he would have refused, but he needed Iset's technical skills, and she knew it.

'The whisper-pipes and the Thinking Mechanisms,' she announced.

'Exactly! The spiderweb of clay tubes that send messages up and down the Nile faster than a horse can run, and the machines waiting to translate and understand those messages.' This was why he needed Iset, a genius with the various contraptions that powered the empire but forbidden from using her genius by dint of her womanhood. That sense of injustice had been the spark Kheti was able to nurse into the flame he needed.

Kheti reached below the table and retrieved a small, elaborately decorated glazed jar. He removed the lid and retrieved another small roll of papyrus. 'The Pharaoh's greatest strength is his ability to know exactly what is going on in his kingdom. A lookout on the Persian border can send a warning and his armies can muster before any invader has even crossed the frontier. If the thinking mechanisms record a shortage of grain in Memphis, a shipment can be sent down the Nile before the first belly begins to grumble.'

'Is this lesson going anywhere?' Ani grumbled. 'Why are we all here, anyway? I was told there was an opportunity to make some silver.'

'It's also his greatest weakness.' Kheti said, ignoring the interruption. 'Anybody who knows how the system works can use it to take what they want right from under his holy nose.

'We're all here because we know how the system works,'

he said, leaning on the table in front of him. 'We're here because we're going to steal a fortune.'

'How?'

'Part one is down to our master forger – Meryre…'

~

Administrative Temple of Thebes

Meryre held his head high as he followed the procession of accountant-priests into the Inner Sanctum, bathing in the sunlight reflected off the statues of gold and the intricate copper cases of the Thinking Mechanisms. The machines fascinated Meryre, they always had, even when he had legitimately been an accountant-priest working with them day-in-day-out in the much less impressive temple in Khent-Mim.

He didn't understand how they worked, only that a priest could take the instructions written in hieroglyphs, turn a series of levers and knobs, and the copper machines would turn out instructions in punched papyrus which another Mechanism would read in Memphis or Cairo. He didn't understand how they worked, but he understood their power. No revolt by the slaves or revolution from the masses would come while machines did the thinking for men. He hadn't needed Kheti's convincing on that point.

Shelves upon shelves of glazed ceramic jars waited for rolls of papyrus to be inserted, sealed, and dropped into the clay pipes depending on the Mechanism's instructions. A complicated series of pumps powered by the Nile pushed air – and the whispers – across the Two Kingdoms.

Meryre walked past the rows of scribes carefully translating orders and records into instructions for the knobs and dials of the Thinking Mechanisms and took his place among them, taking a fresh sheet of papyrus and a quill from the ink pot. He glanced at the men around him and retrieved a crudely etched list on a sheet of palm bark. Some of the entries been crossed out with mud, leaving a list of artefacts that he began to inscribe on the papyrus.

'You there,' a deep voice cut across the room, booming to make itself heard over the clattering and tapping of the Thinking Mechanisms. 'Do I know you?'

Meryre looked up to see the Head Priest marching imperiously towards him, men with curved swords flanking him on either side. Meryre did his best to hide the palm bark beneath the sheets of papyrus.

'No, your Grace,' he said, bowing his head. 'I was sent from the temple at Khen-Min to learn the superior penmanship employed by your scribes, sire.'

'I recall no request,' he frowned. '*I* approve every scribe who comes to my temple.'

Meryre offered a silent prayer to Amun-Ra that the Head Priest could not see his heart beating against his ribs.

'I have the approval here, your Grace,' he said, fishing a roll of papyrus to present to the High Priest. 'The Mechanisms will verify it.'

The elderly man took the papyrus in his bony hands and studied it, carefully. Not for the first time, Meryre second-guessed his penmanship. He had practiced this whisper for days and he was sure that it would appear to be a stamp from a Thinking Mechanism, but he knew that if it was fed by the priests into the copper minds, they would see straight through his forgery.

'Shall I ask the priests to verify it, your Grace?' Meryre asked at last, unable to bear the silence. He held out his hand, willing it not to shake. Behind him, the Mechanism Priests continued their labours, feeding instruction after instruction into their instruments.

Eventually, painfully, the High Priest lowered the forged identity into Meryre's hand.

'No, the instruction is clear, and there is much to be done. Carry on, scribe.'

'Yes, your Grace!'

When the High Priest finally left, Meryre allowed himself a moment to exhale in exhausted relief before returning to the list of treasures. When he was done, he took the newly penned instruction to the priests operating the Mechanisms.

'This is from the Royal Jewellers,' he told the priest. 'Be careful with it.'

'Strange,' the young priest said. 'This is the second instruction from the Jewellers today.'

'Well,' Meryre bluffed. 'The Jubilee festival is coming soon; you wouldn't begrudge our great Pharaoh a great treasure for the day?'

'Of course not!' the priest babbled and took the instruction and began to code it into the Mechanism. When he was done, he turned the wheel, and a dizzying array of cogs and sprockets began to spin. Eventually, a papyrus emerged resplendent in the Mechanism language. The priest took the papyrus and proceeded to the shelves of jars, selecting one, he rolled it inside and was about to send it into the pipes when Meryre shouted out.

'Stop!' the priest turned; hand poised to deliver the false instruction. 'I-I have made a mistake! Please cancel that instruction and let me take another look at the list.'

The priest rolled his eyes and shoved the jar into Meryre's chest.

'This is why we don't deal with Khent-Min clowns. Dispose of this and get it *right* this time.'

'Of course, my deepest apologies!' Meryre bowed deeply and backed out of the inner sanctum, holding the first piece of their plan.

~

A farm outside Thebes

'...I don't understand,' Ani said, interrupting Kheti's description of Meryre's role. 'If what you're saying is right then the *true* list of treasures being sent to the temple in Memphis will already be recorded in the Mechanism in Thebes. How does a forgery help us?'

Kheti's eyes shimmered in the lamplight, and he gestured to the map.

'When the boatload of sacred treasures leaves Thebes, it will be stopped to be blessed by the priests in Abydos. Now, it takes a day's sailing from Thebes to Abydos, but the whisper-pipes take only a few hours, which means that the priests there will know exactly what to expect.'

Meryre leaned in, barely restraining the grin on his face.

'They'll check the list on-board and make two copies of the instructions – one sent back to Thebes and the other to the final destination in Memphis,' he explained. 'The accountant priests will feed those instructions back into the Thinking Mechanisms and the transfer will be complete. If anybody stops the boat after leaving Abydos, the theft will be spotted when they check the list in Memphis.'

'Suddenly all the Pharaoh's forces will be alerted, and guards will be checking every horse, camel, and boat from Kush to the Mediterranean.' Kheti announced, slapping his hand on the map to make his point.

'But that's only if the lists don't match.'

Ani frowned; clearly his brain had never been the ex-chariot racer's most important attribute.

'The list that Meryre will fabricate will be a list of everything we *leave behind* after we've carried out the heist while the boat is docked in Abydos – after the priests have already sent their whisper back to Thebes to confirm everything is in place.'

'So, we send our message after we've nicked the loot?'

'No, because at that point the original list will already be on its way through the pipes to Memphis,' Kheti grinned, and pointed to a spot in the desert. 'Which is where Iset and her little sister come into play…'

~

An hour downriver of Abydos

'I thought that you said you knew where it was?' Tiye – the little sister in question – asked as they crossed the same wheat field again.

'I did… I *do*,' Iset corrected herself as she scanned the ground. 'Only the last time I found it, it was shortly after the floods receded and there was nothing in the field but mud. Not to mention that I wasn't searching by moonlight.'

'It's after midnight, the priests must have already sent the whisper by now,' Tiye said.

'Don't you think that I know that?' Iset snapped. 'Look, this is the only place for leagues around where the whisper-pipes aren't being guarded by watchtowers. It's the only place with a pump hidden behind those hills, it must be here somewhere. Instead of complaining, why don't you help look?'

'I *am* looking,' Tiye insisted from the back of her agitated horse. 'I'm also keeping a lookout for soldiers.'

Iset shook her head and returned to prowling through the wild grass at the edge of the wheat-field. Suddenly, she became aware of a strange sound in the distance and looked to Tiye who had also heard it and was scanning the dark horizon. What was that sound? Not a horse's hooves or the rattle of a chariot's wheel. It was a wheezing, knocking sound…

The whisper-pipe!

Iset dived into the mud and put her ear to the ground, listening to the vibrations. She held up a hand to hush her sister and darted into the grass before dropping to the ground again.

'Got you!'

The clay pipe had been buried under heaps of rotting reeds deposited by the earlier floods. She called to Tiye and the two dug out and exposed the rough, solid surface. With a direction to follow, they were able to trace the line of the pipe to behind an outcropping where the air pump wheezed and groaned. Suddenly the entire contraption stood out to her as though emblazoned in gold; there was the pipe! There the axle leading down to the river where a distant wheel turned, providing the power to make the bulky collection of wood, copper, clay, and animal skins keep blowing fresh air into the pipe.

'Iset!'

She had gotten distracted, and now they could both hear the distinctive rattle as a whisper-jar shot through the pipe, pushed along by the previous pump. Iset swore and brought her hoe down on the pipe, which deflected it without trouble. The rattling grew louder and Iset attacked the ceramic like a woman possessed, cracks began to form as the jar inside the pipe got closer and closer.

Smash.

The pipe shattered and Iset was instantly blinded by a plume of sand and soil as the pressure inside burst out. She backed away, satisfied, but when she looked at Tiye, she clocked the wide-eyed expression of horror in her little sister's eyes.

The pipe was still rattling.

She had missed the jar. The next pump heaved, and she knew that it was being pushed along out of their reach. Iset thought quickly, crudely sketched diagrams flashing in her mind as she tried to find a way to salvage the situation.

'Tiye!' she shouted. 'Get the horse to trample the link to the pump. There! Do it now!'

Tiye didn't protest, she yanked the horse's reigns and ordered it to the delicate pipe connecting the waterwheel in the river with the pump. The horse reared and its mass of muscles and sinew dropped on the linkage which shattered instantly. The broken mouth of the pipe gave one final burp before the pump went totally still. Tiye brought the horse back around to her sister.

'Now what?'

~

Abydos

A few hours earlier, Ani and Kheti watched from behind reeds as an ornate sailboat glided down the Nile, the setting sun glittering in the golden stitching in the sails and flashing off the curved swords of the soldiers along the length of the rail. Lesser craft parted before it, splashing oars to make way for the effortlessly elegant vessel cutting through the water towards the Royal Warehouse.

Like every royal building in Abydos, the Warehouse groaned under the weight of intricately carved statues, murals which shone in the setting sun, and decorations from the edge of the roof to even the wooden stilts plunged confidently into the mud and sand of the Nile. At the booming of a drum on board the boat, the sail was brought down, and bronzed servants hauled open two monstrous wooden doors guarding the entrance to the Warehouse. The boat slipped inside, and the doors closed with the roar of a dragon swallowing its prey.

'Sunset,' Ani grunted as the sun finally dipped beneath the temple-studded horizon of Abydos. 'Bang on time.'

'I told you,' Kheti said. 'The Thinking Mechanisms ensure everything runs to time. It's just one more reason that we couldn't have intercepted the boat between Memphis and here. If it didn't arrive when the Mechanisms here said it would, the alarm would be raised.'

'So instead, we steal it from under the nose of an entire platoon of the Pharoah's guard?' Ani said, his eyes darting to the gleaming bronze swords held by men on the pier beside the Warehouse, the two stood atop it like carrion birds, more in front of the foot entrance, and the ones they saw occasionally patrolling back and forth on the road behind it.

'If we do this right, they'll never see us coming,' Kheti winked. 'Come on; let's get started while we have a little bit of light left.'

Kheti rustled his way through the reeds back to where a strange bundle was hidden beneath a rough tarp. He unveiled the bamboozling collection of wood, sheepskin, and pipes as though revealing a great treasure which, he supposed, in a way it was.

'Are you sure that this contraption is going to work?' the charioteer asked, as he set to work assembling the mass of objects into their means of getting in and out of the warehouse.

'I have absolute confidence in Iset's inventions.'

'Why should I share that confidence?'

Kheti sighed and turned away from the half-assembled device.

'Because she sacrificed a comfortable, easy life to do this,' he said. 'I overheard merchants laughing about the mad woman from Giza trying to sell inventions in the marketplace. The royal guard put a stop to it every time, but every day she would go back, having rebuilt the smashed devices overnight. She needs this plan to work to make a life for her and her sister.'

'I still don't understand why she's safely out in the desert while we're risking our necks,' Ani grunted, inserting a pipe into a wooden box covered with folded sheepskin.

'We're *all* risking our lives doing this,' Kheti growled, stopping in his own construction work. 'We need each of us at every stage to make this work.'

'Even the kid?' Ani replied with one eyebrow raised. 'I can't believe she's getting an equal share.'

'We're *all* needed.'

Ani simply grunted in response.

By the time they had finished, night had begun to set, and a constellation of torches burst into life across Abydos. The pair hauled the bizarre contraption through the reeds and into the shallow waters of the Nile just as the door to the Warehouse opened, and a troop of people emerged, led by a priest from the temple. He cast a quick spell of protection on the door and left, leaving the Warehouse to be guarded by the solid slab of muscle and bronze at the door.

'All right, are you ready?' Kheti asked, as he took the box with sheepskin under one arm and brought the end of the attached pipe to his mouth. Ani didn't reply, but Kheti could see in his eyes that he was terrified. He took the pipe out of his mouth and placed a hand on his sweating shoulder to reassure him. 'Remember, try to breathe.'

Ani placed the hose in his mouth, nodded, and then they both began to wade out into the Nile. Silt gripped at Kheti's feet as the cold water lapped up and around him. By the time they reached the edge of the reeds, the waster was already chilling his belly. He held up a hand and counted down from three… two… one…

They sank beneath the surface, plunged into a cold world of darkness and claustrophobia. For a moment, Kheti panicked, every instinct in his body wanted to force him up to the surface and the refreshing air just above them. Instead, he tried to calm himself, easing his breathing and starting to gently pump the waxed sheepskin bellows under his arm. Iset had designed the pump similarly to the machines which sent the whispers through the desert, just scaled down to deliver gulps of air through a pipe disguised as a reed just above the surface.

The bank of the Nile slipped away beneath them, and they began to swim, awkwardly and unevenly at first, then they found their rhythm, kicking gently to propel themselves forward while Kheti pumped the bellows. The silty Nile water rendered them both virtually blind, with only the dull orange glow of the Warehouse's torches guiding them forwards.

Kheti's heart pounded, wishing that he could surface and check where they were, or even lift his ear out to make sure that they hadn't been seen, but the water that rendered them virtually deaf and blind also hid them from the piercing eyes of the soldiers.

Suddenly there was a bump, the breathing pipe had hit *something* on the surface. Kheti froze, he felt a hand on his arm, Ani was gesturing for him to look up, even through the murk of the water he could see that much. Above them, the world was neatly cut into a sickly orange glow of torchlight and utter, total darkness. The pipe had hit the Warehouse door. Kheti breathed a sigh of relief, sucking down more river water than he had intended.

He coughed.

He tried to hold it back, but his lungs betrayed him, spluttering in protest at the foul muddy water coating his throat. Before he could stop him, Kheti found Ani's strong arm wrapped around his waist as he gave a powerful kick and forced them under the door and into the Warehouse.

Kheti kicked for the surface, needing fresh air, and emerged into a totally still pool of ink-black water lit only by a pair of ceremonial torches left burning on the boat above them. Ani followed shortly after and for a moment they simply floated in the shadow of the treasure-boat, waiting for the shouts of soldiers and the pounding of sandaled feet.

Nothing came.

'What the hell was that about?' Ani hissed. *'You could have gotten us both killed!'*

'I swallowed some river-water, I couldn't help it.' Kheti whispered back, trying to regain control of the situation. *'Look, we're in now, we don't have time to argue.'*

Ani glowered at Kheti, His eyes burned with reflected torchlight, but he pursed his lips and helped lift the breathing gear out of the water.

Kheti's eyes were now firmly fixed on the gangplank leading onto the treasure-ship. He hurried on-board without even a glance back, his breathing shallow and pulse racing. Ani followed behind him and together they approached the chest in the middle of the deck. Made of polished ebony, set with precious jewels, and carved with scenes from the great lineage of Pharaohs, the box itself was worth more than Kheti would ever own in his life. He grinned like a crocodile.

'Remember,' Kheti said, breathlessly placing his hands on the lid of the chest. *'We have a list; they're the only things that we*

steal.'

'I know the plan…'

Kheti pushed and the lid opened with a sigh of trapped Theban air. Even in the low light of the warehouse, the innards glistened. Gold and precious stones sparkled at them, seeming to invite them to reach in and take them.

Kheti looked at Ani. Ani looked at Kheti. Kheti bit his lip.

Then they dived into the box, both unable to pull themselves away from the tantalising treasures worth more than their lives. Kheti's hands trembled as he plucked a heavy gold necklace dripping with rubies and sapphires. He could work an honest life until Osiris weighed his heart, and he would never earn enough to so much as touch such a treasure.

He placed it over his head.

Meanwhile, Ani had adorned his fingers with so many golden rings set with precious stones that his hands clicked like crickets.

Eventually, Kheti sighed and removed the necklace from his neck – it was too heavy, too unwieldy, and not on the list.

'Come on, we've got work to do.'

They began to methodically sort through the chest, picking out pre-selected pieces – those that were small, but valuable, those not part of a set, or that would be missed by a particularly fussy priest. Plates and dishes were easy choices, crowns and jars less so. By the time that they were finished laying their haul out on a sheet of sodden linen, the chest still appeared achingly full – surely one more ring wouldn't be missed? Surely, they could pry just *one* glistening stone from the constellation embedded into this or that necklace?

Kheti shut the lid, hiding the temptations from their lecherous eyes. They both sighed as they took their meagre haul – only enough to make them fabulously wealthy for life – and brought the ends of the linen together, forming the fabric into a tight bundle. Suddenly, as one solid mass of precious metal, the weight of their collection hit them, and they staggered down the gangplank back towards the pumps lying beside the water.

They set to work as they had practiced, stringing rope through the open gaps of the linen, tying it to a waterproof goat-hide bag connected to a pump. As the stronger of the pair of them, Ani began to squeeze the bellows, forcing air into the goatskin while Kheti lowered himself, and the rest of the equipment into the water.

A sound caused them both to freeze, the sliding of a wooden bar and the creaking of a door. Ani and Kheti looked at each other with wide eyes, and then turned to the entrance on the opposite side of the water. Light flooded in from a torch held aloft by a soldier with his hand on his sword.

'Hurry! Get in!' Kheti hissed, knowing that if they were so much as spotted, the plan would unravel. Ani didn't need telling twice, he carefully lowered the goatskin balloon into the water before lowering himself down. As he dropped his hand, a ring set with amethyst slipped from his finger. Kheti watched it fall in slow motion, unable to do anything from the water.

The ring hit the sandstone like a gong, echoing throughout the warehouse. It bounced, bounced again, then slipped beneath the inky black water with a damning splash.

The footsteps of the patrolling guard stopped, then the torch was held aloft as he began to hunt for the source of the noise.

Kheti glowered at Ani, but said nothing, instead handing him a breathing tube and let out just enough air from the goatskin that it vanished beneath the surface. He donned his own breathing tube and dived. The two swam for their lives, legs kicking away clumsily and desperately, trying not to disturb the water. They could see nothing through the murk, not knowing whether they were about to be spotted by the waiting guard.

All the while, the vision of the stolen ring falling from Ani's finger played itself on a loop in Kheti's mind.

~

A farm outside Thebes

Several days later, Iset, Meryre, and Tiye waited in silence as the hours trickled by. Occasionally the older sister would find the nervous energy too much to contain and begin to pace around the little farmhouse, but they never said a word between them. It was if by speaking they could break the spell holding the world in a consequence-free limbo. The world was a flipped medallion, hanging in the air by the sheer force of will of their silence – if they broke it, the medallion would land, and they would discover their fate.

'How long do we wait?' Meryre's words were quiet, nearly whispered, but against the agonising silence they were like the ringing of a temple bell. Iset couldn't answer him, instead she simply shook her head and dropped onto a bench.

She yelped as a series of knocks at the door shattered the silence that Meryre had strained. Iset gestured for her little sister to hide, as she drew a bronze dagger and crept to the door. She licked lips as dry as papyrus and offered up a silent prayer to Osiris. With her free hand, she shunted back the bolt on the door and pulled back the door, her left hand ready to strike like a cobra.

When she saw Kheti's face, she dropped the knife and threw open the door. Iset laughed and threw her arms around the man whose clothes were stained with the mud of the Nile, sand and dust caked his face and hair, and his eyes spoke of a long and wearying ride.

'You're alive!' she laughed.

'So am I, if anyone cares,' Ani smiled as he followed behind Kheti, arms burdened with a dirty linen wrap around an uneven shape.

'You did it?' Tiye squeaked.

Ani dropped the bundle triumphantly and the wrap opened like a lotus flower to reveal a glittering hoard of gold. Iset's hands went to her mouth while Tiye squealed and Meryre fell to his knees in disbelief. Kheti stood sullen and glowering at the charioteer.

'What happened?' Iset asked, seeing the stormy face on the mastermind.

'Ani here couldn't help himself.'

'It was *one ring*!' Ani protested, as if this was an argument they had had over and over again. 'You saw that chest; nobody is going to notice…'

'*It was a treasure from the Royal Jewellers!*' Kheti exploded, squaring up to the larger man's chest. 'Do you think that they're casual about the whereabouts of holy relics? Do you think that I planned all this to throw it away because you got greedy?'

'Don't get sanctimonious, we're all greedy, we're all thieves, at least I'm honest.'

'This isn't about greed, it's about my…' Kheti took a breath to collect himself. 'This isn't about greed, for anyone but you.'

Ani shrugged.

'By the time they notice, we'll be long gone,' he said, pushing past the mastermind and addressing Iset directly. 'As long as you pulled off your end of the operation? One ring can easily go missing, but we took far more than one ring.'

Iset and Tiye exchanged a glance between them and Iset felt her lips dry up again.

'What happened?'

~

An hour downriver of Abydos

The first glimmers of dawn played across the sky as Iset and Tiye worked to correct their mistake. They had broken the pipe again just ahead of the jar and were now scrabbling to replace the break with the prepared length of clay pipe they had loaded onto the horse. Iset swore as the sun began to chase away their covering darkness, keenly aware of the potential eyes from the watchtower just visible over the crest of the hill.

'That feels tight,' Iset said to Tiye, giving the connection a final shove. 'Try pumping it now.'

Tiye grabbed the end of the bellows of the broken pump and jumped, letting her slight bodyweight pull the surface down. Iset held her breath, Tiye tried again. If there was a leak, the air would do nothing, and it would not take long for people to notice that the flow of whispers had ceased and send people to investigate. Tiye jumped again, this time, there was a rattle, and the jar inside began to move. Iset held back the urge to shout out and instead simply fell back on the dusty ground to let out a sigh of relief. She allowed herself to indulge in that feeling for a moment, before she stumbled to her feet and made her way back to where her sister was sweatily pumping, grabbed the bellows, and began to lend her own strength.

'Go... back to the break... in the pipe,' she grunted, through pumps. 'Check to see if there are any more jars waiting to be sent through.'

'I don't understand.'

'We can't fix this pipe, or the pump, I don't have the tools,' she explained, now thoroughly in her rhythm. 'Eventually, they'll send somebody to investigate the break, they might think it's an accident, or they might conclude sabotage, either way, they'll be suspicious of the first whisper that went through the pipes. If we send more through...'

Tiye fished out jars and sent them through the pipe until the sun appeared on the horizon and farmers began their day along the Nile. By the time Iset said that it was enough, she was drenched in sweat and coated with sand and dirt. Tiye's hands were grazed and cut, and her knees were bloody from crouching on the ground.

'Come on, we need to go meet the others.'

~

A farm outside Thebes

The others in question exploded at the news. Ani immediately confronted Iset, demanding to know if that meant that they were compromised. Meryre gripped his hair and began pacing around the enclosed space, saying 'no, no, no,' over and over. Tiye confronted Ani, shouting at him to leave her big sister alone. Meanwhile, Kheti dropped heavily on a bench, gripping his mouth and staring into the middle-distance. The fight continued until Ani pushed Iset aside and began to throw treasures haphazardly into the linen sheet, telling the others that he was leaving, assuring them that he would see them all in Athens or Roma if the soldiers didn't stop them first.

'How long does it take to sail from Memphis to Thebes?' Kheti asked, eventually. The squabbling group halted in their arguing, disarmed by the incongruous question.

'A week, maybe six days if the winds are blowing well,' Meryre answered.

'We managed to get the whisper into the pipes. It will be at least a day until somebody notices that there are no messages coming, then they'll have to find the break, *then* they'll have to think it's suspicious,' Kheti began listing his points while pointing to his fingers for emphasis. 'Finally, they have to find all the whispers sent on the night of the break, check them all, and verify them with their sender. Assuming that Meryre's forgeries are good enough, it'll pass through the check at Abydos – apart from Ani's ring – and only be noticed when it reaches the jewellers at Thebes.

'By my reckoning, that gives us just over a week to make sure that all this is *gone* – melted down and turned into something less conspicuous.' He walked over to Ani and grabbed the sheet off him. 'We stick to the plan; we just have to be quick about it and hope that they blame the ring on a sticky-fingered slave in Memphis.'

'Meryre, are the casts ready for the gold? Good. Iset, get that forge fired up and this gold melted down. Tiye, help your sister. Ani, get in touch with your contacts, tell them that we'll be ready to move sooner than expected. I'll keep my ear to the ground, find out just what the Pharaoh knows.'

He clapped his hands and the group jumped to their feet, scrambling to turn the highly distinctive jewellery into anonymous, unremarkable coinage. As Kheti walked through the door, he felt a rough hand on his shoulder.

'You always said that it was foolish to talk about spending money that we don't have,' Ani said. 'But people talk. I'm planning on funding my way back into chariot racing, Iset wants a workshop to make new inventions, Meryre has his political ambitions, but what do *you* get out of this?'

~

Rahenu Mine

The smell of dust baked under the oppressive sun sent a shiver down Kheti's spine. He could feel it caking the back of his throat, sticking to his hair, and felt as if every warm breeze was stripping away the years of disguise he had spent cultivating since he was last at Rahenu. He tried to stop his feet from bouncing nervously as he waited for the foreman to appear, suddenly feeling very alone. The rest of the crew had scattered, gone into hiding up and down the Nile until the wrath of the Pharaoh died down.

But Kheti had one last part of the plan to see through.

'I am sorry to keep you waiting, sir,' the voice cut through Kheti. Even dulled with age and carrying the manners of equals, there was no mistaking the rumbles which could become a roar when barking orders and wielding a whip.

'Please,' Kheti said, gesturing for the man to join him beneath the shade. The foreman thanked him and settled onto the bench opposite, his sharp features not blunted by time – if anything the sun had baked his skin into taut leather, giving him the look of a scabbard holding a blade.

'I understand you're in the market for slaves?' he began.

'*A* slave,' Kheti corrected him. 'I sent a whisper through the pipes concerning the particular individual I'm looking for.'

The foreman held himself upright, his forehead folding into a frown.

'Yes, I received it. I have to say that it's an odd request. I have many hundreds of fine workers, why this one? He is lame in one leg, the accident that killed his brother also made him sullen, wilful, and resentful.'

'In that case, the price I offered should be more than ample compensation,' Kheti said, pulling out a leather purse filled to bursting with newly minted gold.

The foreman studied Kheti, his sharp eyes narrowing as he considered the man sitting opposite him. Slowly, he began to nod.

'I know you, don't I?' he said, then the corner of his

mouth cracked into a cruel smile. Kheti remained silent, hoping that the beads of sweat appearing on his forehead were mistaken for perspiration in the mid-day heat. 'So, the accident didn't kill you after all. I should take that gold as compensation for years of missed labour and have my whip-holders send you back down the shafts.'

'My associates know I'm here,' Kheti lied. 'More importantly, the Royal Records know that I died ten years ago. You reported it for the tax relief. Reporting false information to the accountant-priests carries a hefty penalty – are you prepared to risk it for one slave over his prime? Just take the treasure and let my brother go.'

The foreman scrutinised Kheti's face, his eyes mining for information like a pick. Eventually, his lip curled, and he held his hand up to click his fingers.

'You're right, the both of you are more trouble than you're worth.'

Kheti didn't hear him, instead, he was transfixed by the skeletal man blinking in the sunlight as he was hauled from a storage shed to be presented like a pack mule. When he had last seen his brother, he had been built like an ox, now those muscles had withered and the strong beard had become a straggly tangle of hairs, but the recognition between the two of them was immediate. Kheti jumped to his feet and raced to embrace him.

In the Administrative Temple of Thebes, the forged whisper had been discovered, but Kheti wouldn't have cared even if he'd known. He had recovered his real treasure.

The Plan

Tessa was at home when she got the call. Just two words, but she knew what they meant, knew the heartbreak behind them, knew the reluctance and the fear that motivated them.

'It's time.'

'Shit,' she sighed. 'All right, are you at the flat? Give me twenty minutes.'

She put the phone down before her friend could thank her, or apologise, or change her mind. Instead, she grabbed a coat, her keys, and her wallet and walked quickly to her old Vauxhall Corsa. She didn't run, didn't want to get her heartbeat going or put sweat on her brow. Lexis needed to see that she was calm, in control, ready to put The Plan into action even if she wasn't.

When Tessa pulled up outside the low-rise block of 1980s flats, her heart sank. Lexis was sat on the wall with her belongings stuffed into the two suitcases they had picked out together when they had started formulating The Plan, her cheeks puffy and stained by recent tears, and her suit dishevelled and crumpled. Worst of all was her hair – shorn short in the style that she hated but was a necessary part of getting by in boymode. When she saw the Corsa pull up, she gave Tessa a furtive wave and a fleeting smile.

'Hey,' Tessa said, unrolling the driver's side window by hand. 'Do you need a hand with the bags?'

'No,' she sobbed, grabbing the handle of the larger bag. 'I just can't believe—'

'Not here,' Tessa interrupted her. 'Tell me what happened when we hit the road. The boot is open.'

The two bags barely fit in the Corsa's little boot but soon they were pulling away, leaving Lexis to stare at her home – her former home – in the rear-view mirror. They sat in silence while they navigated through the busy Birmingham streets toward the motorway, slowed by the fleets of parents picking up their children from school. Only when they were safely on the left-hand lane of the M6 heading north did Lexis finally allow herself a shuddering sigh.

'Thank you for this, Tess. I have all the details written down,' she said at last, putting a folded piece of paper into the drink holders. 'I'm sorry, I know you would have had plans, things that—'

'—hey, the only plan that matters now is The Plan, all right? Apologise again and I'll dump you at the next set of services, deal?'

Lexis smiled.

'Deal.'

'So, what happened?'

'Someone saw me out of boymode,' Lexis replied. 'I thought I recognised one of them in Tesco the other night, but hoped… well…'

'A kid from your class?' Tess asked, trying to work out whether one of the little shits had dobbed her in as revenge for a bad report card.

'I don't think so, David didn't say who, only that he'd received a report from "a concerned parent" and under the new legislation he'd have to follow it up to the Police. Oh, and that I would be terminated, of course.'

'Bastard.'

'It's not his fault,' Lexis sighed. 'What else could he do? If it ever came out that he didn't follow it up the government could shut the school down, fire everyone who knew, and put it under new management.'

Tessa shook her head, intellectually she had always known that this was a risk, how many times had she and Lexis discussed it, argued about it, but to be faced with the reality of it made her want to burn something.

'Did he at least say how long he would give you?' Tessa asked through gritted teeth.

'Close-of-play. He's going to tell the office staff before they go home, it's the latest he can leave it – legally I mean.'

Tessa checked the clock on the dashboard, four-thirty-two.

'…and when do…'

'Five, half-five, latest.'

'So, on the bright side, you're probably not a fugitive for another hour,' Tessa snorted, bitterly. Lexis smiled, but it was brief and soon her head was in her hands.

'A fugitive,' she sobbed. 'For what? Living my life. When the government changed, I thought things would be different, but even so, I did everything they asked of me, I put on a suit, cut my hair, hung my dead name from my lanyard like a fucking albatross, wore *this* thing.'

She leaned forward in her seat and reached under her shirt, there was a click and Lexis struggled out of the suffocating confines of her chest binder and tossed it into the footwell. She chuckled.

'Imagine telling me three years ago that the progesterone would have such an effect that I'd even *need* to wear a binder to do boymode,' she sat back in the seat and let her head rest on the cool glass of the window. 'I did all of that just so that I could stay in teaching. With every new law, I put up with it for the sake of the kids.'

'And every time, I told you to get out of here,' said Tess. 'You could've gotten a job anywhere…'

'…anywhere?' Lexis asked with her eyebrow raised.

'All right, not *anywhere,* but Belgium, Spain, Ireland…'

'On the plus side, now you get to say: "I told you so!"'

'That isn't what I meant, I…' Tessa began, but Lexis was smiling.

'Anyway, this is my home. I wasn't about to just leave unless I had to. I guess the time has finally come.'

They drove along in silence for a while as they left the choking traffic of the M6 and headed through the Shropshire hills on the smaller A-roads. Tessa glanced at her friend from time to time, but her attention was set somewhere over the green hills out of the passenger-side window. Tessa could only imagine what was going on in Lexis' head – although The Plan had been prepared over years, it had always seemed distant, remote – like making a bucket list in your early twenties – suddenly they were faced with the reality of putting it into action and making it real.

'David will have told the others by now,' Lexis said, without turning away from the endless fields of cows. 'He'll have gathered the office staff together, told them as gently as he could, then assured them that *he* would be the one to call the police. Pam will have already sent the automated mailer; Yvonne will have updated the records. With a few clicks, Mister Reed, Primary School Teacher will be gone, replaced by Mister Reed, Wanted Sexual Deviant.'

'Well, that's all right, then,' Tessa replied, jauntily. Lexis did a double-take as if she couldn't believe what she was hearing. Tessa smiled. 'Because I'm sat with a Miss Reed, Ferry Passenger… I assume that you *did* book the ticket under *Miss* Reed, right?'

'That's still what it says on my passport. Thank you, ten-year expiration dates!' she announced, proudly waving her passport in the air like Neville Chamberlain declaring "peace in our time."

A road sign advertised a service station ahead and out of habit, Tessa glanced at the fuel gauge. A little less than a quarter of a tank remained, probably enough to get them up to Holyhead, but her old car wasn't as reliable as it once was.

'In that case, the people on the Ferry are going to be expecting to see a *Miss* Reed, I need to pull in for petrol, why don't I fill up while you go and put the boymode away?'

'But what if—' Lexis stopped herself, stopped the automatic moment of fear and doubt that crept in whenever anybody suggested being public – what if she was clocked and reported? Well, now she knew the answer, she could be reported, lose her job, and be made a wanted criminal, but since all that had already happened, why continue hiding from mirrors? 'All right, and we can pick up some snacks, too. I'm starving.'

Tessa guided the Corsa into a small service station squatting on the corner of a roundabout and found a free pump. Lexis hopped out of the car and grabbed a bag from the boot, promising that she would see her inside.

As Tessa unhooked the pump nozzle, she couldn't help watching her friend go with a smile on her face at the way she practically skipped inside. She realised that boymode was more than just the clothes on Lexis' back, the harsh crop of her hair, and letting her voice fall deeper, it was the way she held herself. When she was in boymode, she kept her shoulders square and her movements stiff, but as soon as she shed that, it was as though she were being held aloft with helium balloons.

She shook her head and began filling the fuel tank while Lexis made her way into the disabled toilet and discarded her male-coded attire like a cocoon. Eventually, the pump clicked off, she re-hung the handle and Tessa went inside to grab a bag of crisps and sweets before joining the long line of motorists waiting in line to pay the elderly cashier behind a sheet of plexiglass. While she waited, shuffling forward every minute or so, she scrolled through the ferry times, the shipping forecast for the Irish Sea before nervously opening the news app. She flicked past the first few headlines before tapping into the search bar.

Trans teacher brought up a number of stories about teachers who had been fired and arrested for breaching the Preventing Gender Confusion in Minors Act, none of them from today. *Trans school* brought up a recent case where parents had been taken to court for allowing their child to come into school wearing boys' clothes and using a masculine name. A few more searches brought up similar horror stories, but nothing about Lexis and she breathed a sigh of relief that even if the police knew about her, the press hadn't sniffed it out. Yet.

The line eventually deposited Tessa to the front of the queue. She dropped the bags of snacks onto the counter and told the cashier her pump number.

'That will be eighty-four-sixty, please, love,' said the cashier.

'I'll get this,' Lexis appeared beside her, about to tap her debit card on the machine. Tessa reacted instantly, slapping her hand away from the machine and sending the card skittering onto the floor.

'No, don't worry, I've got this,' Tessa said, hurriedly, and tapped her own card on the screen. The cashier was giving her a suspicious look, which Tessa tried to disarm with a smile. As soon as the check mark appeared on the screen, she grabbed the snacks and took Lexis by the arm as soon as she had retrieved her card, breaking into something between a quick walk and a run. When the automatic door slid closed behind them, Lexis yanked her arm out from Tessa's grip.

'What the hell was that about?' Lexis snapped.

'You were about to use your bank card,' Tessa replied. When that seemed an insufficient explanation, she sighed. 'They can track when you use your card, if the police are looking to track you down, do you think that they're going to need Inspector Poirot on the case to work out why you might be buying fuel at the Welsh border?'

Lexis' cheeks flared bright red even through the light application of foundation she had applied, almost perfectly matching her rosy lips. She casually tossed aside a strand of mahogany hair from the wig which now sat neatly on her head and once again Tessa was struck by how much she physically transformed when she wasn't hiding behind the mask of boymode, even the subtle movements of her head and the positioning of her hands had changed.

'You didn't have to slap the card out of my hand,' she mumbled.

'I know, I'm sorry about that,' Tessa smiled apologetically. 'It was the first thing I thought of to stop you.'

'Other people use their words,' Lexis said with a smile. The tension was gone.

'You look nice, by the way.'

Lexis laughed.

'Nice way to change the topic, you mean?'

'I don't know *what* you're talking about. Come on, we've still got a long trip ahead of us.'

Lexis tossed her bag of male clothes in the boot and slid into the passenger seat, looking infinitely more comfortable in high-rise jeans and a strappy white top than the crumpled suit she had met her in. Suddenly, she went stiff, and the colour drained from her face, Tessa followed her gaze to the police car pulling into the service station.

'Stay calm,' said Tessa, as much to herself as Lexis. 'We don't know why they're here; they're probably just filling up.'

The car pulled into a parking space in front of the entrance and two uniformed officers stepped out and seemed to scan the forecourt.

'Drive,' muttered Lexis. 'Drive. Drive. Drive. Drive. Drive.'

'Calm down.'

'*Drive!*'

Tessa fought the urge to gun the engine and wheelspin out of the forecourt, instead, she held her breath steady and eased the Corsa out onto the road, her eyes constantly flicking back to the two officers who had entered the shop. She didn't let herself let out a breath of relief until the service station was long behind them and vanished from the rear-view mirror.

'That was too close,' Lexis breathed out. 'No more stops until we get to Holyhead. Please. I need to get out of this country.'

'No arguments from me.'

Usually, the towering peaks of Snowdonia, with their snow-covered caps and whisps of clouds hanging off their summits calmed Tessa, promising quiet and isolation from the stresses of ordinary life, but as they drove through the valleys of their foothills Tessa couldn't escape the feeling that they were closing in on them, blocking off their escape and funnelling them into a trap. Instead of considering the sleepy villages nestled in the valleys, she thought about how few roads there were for them to take. It didn't help that dusk was quickly drawing in and the sun kept getting eclipsed by the mountains, throwing them into shadow.

The snacks went uneaten and there was silence between them again until they crossed the Brittania Bridge onto the island of Anglesey.

'Goodbye Great Britain,' Lexis declared as they crossed the box bridge and left the British mainland.

'Maybe you can claim asylum on Anglesey instead,' Tessa joked.

'Maybe once they declare independence from the rest of Wales.'

'Why wait, be the revolution you want to see in the world!'

'The British government already want to lock me up, I'm not sure that adding 'attempted revolutionary' to my charge sheet is going to help me! Anyway, it's a four-hour drive to Anglesey, you can get a flight to Dublin in an hour from Birmingham.'

'Don't remind me,' Tessa groaned, stretching her back from the long drive. 'If the airports were as lax around passport checks as the ferry port is, I wouldn't have had to spend a full tank of petrol driving you out to the arse-end of nowhere.'

'Don't jinx it,' Lexis said, suddenly serious again. 'I know the last couple of times, they've barely bothered to glance at our passports, but all it takes is to have one jobsworth on duty…'

'I know.'

The Plan was mostly ironclad, they already had contact with a human rights lawyer in Dublin ready to meet Lexis and help her through her asylum claim; amongst the bags were reams of documentation and evidence to present to the Irish authorities. The problem was getting to Irish soil to make the claim.

Neither of them knew when the call would be made to the Police to update their records and block Lexis' passport, and there were too many checks at the airports by too many men with guns.

But the ferry was different, half the time, when they had gone to visit friends in the past, they had been simply waved through the little security booth, the bored operative inside relying on the automatic numberplate scanners to make his job easier. When they made The Plan, there had been no question about the route they would take – Holyhead to Dublin.

With every tunnel cut through the craggy rock of Anglesey bringing them closer to the port, the tension in the air seemed to grow until Tessa would have sworn that she could hear both of their hearts beating. She glanced down at the steering wheel; her knuckles were white from gripping the worn plastic. She took a deep breath and made a conscious effort to ease her grip.

'You—*we* need to relax,' she said at last, cutting the cord of tension so suddenly that Lexis actually jumped in her seat. 'Remember, we're supposed to be going on holiday. We don't want to give them any reason to be suspicious.'

'I can't help it,' Lexis admitted. 'I just keep running scenarios through my mind – what if there are police there waiting for us? What if they search our bags and find the suit my boymode stuff? What if…'

To Lexis' surprise, Tessa burst out laughing.

'*That's* what you're worried about?' She laughed. 'Look, babe, I don't want to burst your bubble, but you're not a terrorist or an escaped murderer. The police aren't going to be running a national manhunt for you. Worst case scenario is that they've flagged your name with Border Security

Command to keep an eye out for your passport, *that's* what we need to be concerned with. As soon as we're through that little booth, we're home-free.'

'How can you say that?' Lexis responded. 'You know the atmosphere around people like me, you know the paranoia, the hate…'

'My phone is just there,' Tessa said, indicating to the centre console. Lexis looked confused but picked it up. 'I looked you up while you were in the bathroom. You weren't even on the news sites yet.'

Lexis tapped at the screen, bringing up the BBC, local news sites, even some of the more sensational tabloids.

'I know that the amount of noise made about people like you makes it seem like you're the government's number one priority, that they *really* care about "protecting women and children," but it's all for show – none of them really care.'

'Then why do all this? Why spend months putting together The Plan? Why have you spent hours driving me to Wales?'

'Because you're my friend,' Tessa shrugged. 'And because you're still not safe here. They don't really care, but they still made the laws, they'll still send you to prison, because it's easy propaganda; a convenient way for them to pretend to be doing something.

'We don't have to make it easy for them.'

Lexis looked unconvinced, but she didn't say anything as they crossed the final bridge towards the port. Tessa couldn't help thinking how inauspicious a start to Lexis' new life the port represented – in the early dusk light, it was hard to tell the dark grey sea of tarmac from the dark grey of the Irish Sea and the dark grey of the heavily-laden clouds above. On a dark hill beyond the port itself stood a sombre obelisk overlooking the port and the town; a monument dedicated to a skilled ship captain made famous in the town both for campaigning for the rights and conditions of sailors, and for being washed overboard from his ship, the *Escape*.

'Portentous bastard,' Tessa muttered towards the monument. Lexis frowned but didn't press.

The ferry itself shone like a beacon with navigation and running lights, along with a constellation of orange rectangles from the windows. The docking ramps were already lowered and as Tessa guided the Corsa into a queue of cars and caravans waiting to be let on board, a steady stream of vehicles joined the service road going the other way.

'Do you think that will ever be me?' Lexis asked, as they watched the flow of traffic leaving the ferry. 'Feeling safe enough to come back, I mean?'

'I hope not,' Tessa replied. Lexis' jaw dropped and a frown creased her forehead. 'Hey, I'm just saying that it's a long drive. If you come back, I hope it'll be by plane!'

The traffic rolled on and on, leaving those waiting to embark sat long enough to turn their engines off. Eventually, Tessa groaned, released her seatbelt and opened her door, only to find Lexis grabbing her.

'What are you doing?' she hissed.

'Stretching my legs, catching some of that sea breeze,' she replied. 'Joining me?'

Lexis shook her head with her jaw locked tight.

'Suit yourself.'

'Tess. *Tess!*'

Tessa shut the door behind her, and it took less than a minute before the passenger side opened and Lexis emerged, hugging her chest tightly. She walked alongside her friend, shoulders hunched, and head lowered as if making herself small would hide her from the waiting drivers and passengers around them. Tessa placed a hand gently on Lexis' arm.

'It might take a while, but you'll be back,' Tessa said. 'The tide will turn; the laws will change. We'll stand together on British soil again, even if this is the last time for a while.'

The two friends stood leaning against the car, watching the procession of cars and lorries on the other side of the chain-link fence and simply taking in the final evening they would spend together in their home country. Finally, the flow of vehicles slowed to a trickle and the final busload of crew drove down the ramp onto terra firma. Other drivers in the queue noticed and engines began to fire up, others who had been walking around made their way back to their cars.

'Are you ready?' Tessa asked. Lexis' face was pale, and her lips were drawn into a tight line, but she nodded, gave her friend a desperate hug, then they both settled back inside and waited for the queue to start moving towards the border post. They both watched, intensely as each car rolled up to the booth and a uniformed officer took the documents. A few seconds later, he handed them a slip of card to hang from the rear-view mirror.

'It doesn't look like they've stepped up security,' Tessa muttered, as a car loaded with lads and filled up to the roof with luggage was waved through after only a cursory glance at their documents. One by one, they inched towards the head of the queue.

Tessa finally unfolded the slip of paper that her friend hand handed her to check the details. Her usually pin-neat writing was shaky, and there were blotches on the page from tearstains, but she was able to check the ferry times and ticket numbers. She looked up to confirm everything with Lexis, but she was staring wildly out of the front window, visibly hyperventilating. Tessa grabbed her hand that was digging deep trenches into her seat. 'Hey, hey! Relax! Take a deep breath, unclench your hands, count down from one hundred. I'm not having everything fall apart because you couldn't hold it together.'

Lexis bit her lip and nodded; with obvious effort, she lifted her hands and folded them neatly in her lap. She closed her eyes and Tessa watched her lips subtly moving as she counted backwards.

'All right,' Lexis said at last, breathing out and shaking her hands. 'Showtime.'

The car rolled up to the cheaply cladded booth where a bored looking man in his forties or fifties held out a ruddy hand from behind a sliding window.

'Passports,' he said in a heavy north Welsh accent, by way of introduction and instruction. Tessa grabbed the documents and handed them over, already opened to the relevant pages – all to make the process as smooth and painless as possible. He set Lexis' aside and flipped idly through Tessa's mostly empty booklet of entry stamps before returning to the front page, his small eyes flicked between the driver and the photograph before he shrugged and tapped something into his computer.

One down, Tessa thought.

He picked up Lexis' documents and Tessa fought to maintain her poker face, keeping a polite but subdued smile plastered over the well of panic threatening to burst through. Again, he flipped through the document before returning to that front page. He glanced at the photograph, then looked down at the car and Tessa saw the little crease of a confused frown on his bald head.

Shit.

He leaned forwards to better scrutinise the Lexis sat in the passenger seat to the one on her passport photograph –

the one taken a year ago after she had received her gender-recognition certificate – when the progesterone was still doing its work on Lexis' face.

'Can you lean forward, please, Miss Reed?'

To Tessa's surprise, Lexis was smiling when she leaned across her to be better seen by the border guard.

'I keep saying that I need to get a new passport photo taken,' she laughed – only Tessa would have been able to pick up on the undercurrent of nervousness bubbling away underneath it. 'People keep saying that I look like a man in it!'

The officer held Lexis' passport up and compared the two faces side-by-side before he put the document down and turned back to the computer. Tessa and Lexis stole a nervous glance at one another as the silent officer tapped away at the keyboard. In her head, Tessa started counting down from one hundred.

The guard reached down below Tessa's eyeline, and it was as if he was moving in slow-motion, seemingly taking minutes to re-emerge, but when he did, it was with a card hanger and a smile.

'Don't worry about it, Miss, you ought to see my wife's passport photo, bloomin' awful!' Tessa was so shocked that she simply sat there without reaching for the proffered documents and hanger until he shook them slightly. 'You ladies have a good trip, hang this on your mirror; drive around to the left and a colleague will direct you from there.'

'Thank you,' said Tessa, numbly taking the passports and hanger from him before pulling away with a lurch. The two sat in stunned, disbelieving silence as they wound their way through the loading yard before they were stopped by another officer wearing a high-visibility vest and wielding a mirror on the end of a metal pole.

Tessa and Lexis shared a glance that that attempted to reassure them without drawing suspicion from the woman walking towards them.

We've done this before, Tessa tried to convince herself. *They just want to check for contraband, they're not interested in us.* She loosened the grip on the steering wheel and rolled down the window.

'Evening, just need to check around the car, won't be a minute,' she said, with a cheerful lilt.

'I don't think my heart can take much more of this,' Lexis whispered, as Tessa shut the window to keep out the chill air blowing in off the Irish Sea.

'Almost there.'

After what Tessa considered to be a very cursory inspection, they were waved onto a final waiting area where they joined the back of one of five queues waiting to board. She shut off the engine and both slumped back into the seats.

'God, I wish I wasn't driving,' Tessa sighed. 'I could murder a vodka and coke right about now.'

'Make mine a G and T,' Lexis laughed.

'Hey, *you* can! The Duty Free is just over there,' she said, nodding towards a converted steel shipping container. Lexis shook her head.

'I'm not getting out of this car until we're safely on the boat,' Lexis declared.

They waited as the line of cars behind them filtered into the boarding queues, soon the stream of vehicles became a trickle, and finally no more headlights joined them on the slab of concrete. A bus carrying foot passengers was the first to be released to enter the yawning mouth of the ferry and

Tessa turned the ignition when her phone began to ring through the car's wireless connection. Frowning, she looked at the screen, caller ID was from somewhere in the Midlands. Before Lexis could stop her, Tessa's thumb clicked on the green answer call symbol on the steering wheel and the call connected.

'Good evening, is this Miss Theresa Jones?' The voice on the other end of the call was deep, male, and stiff with authority. Tessa glanced at Lexis, who was frozen in her seat.

'Speaking?'

'This is Inspector Mahmoud from West Midlands Police; we're currently searching for a fugitive who we believe may have recently been in contact with you.'

Tessa's mouth went dry, and her thumb hovered over the 'end call' button. Meanwhile, a man in a hi-viz vest began directing their own column of cars up the concrete ramp onto the waiting ship.

'Miss Jones?' the inspector prompted, and Tessa realised that she had said nothing for the best part of a minute.

'Yes, sorry, the connection isn't great,' she said, as the Corsa's wheels left the concrete and settled on the metal bridge connecting the ferry to dry land. 'Did you say that you were looking for a fugitive?'

'That's right, a Mister Reed, we have reason to believe that he may have reached out to you earlier this afternoon.'

Lexis drew a sharp intake of breath, her eyes flicking to the many men and women in uniform so very close to the ferry.

'I'm sorry, I can't help you,' Tessa said, with a confidence that caught Lexis by surprise. 'Nobody with that name has contacted me today, good evening, officer.'

She ended the phone call as the car settled into place on the deck of the ferry. As soon as she switched the engine off, Lexis leapt across the handbrake to wrap her arms around her.

'Thank you, thank you!' she gushed. 'You didn't have to do that, if they found out that you lied to a Police officer…'

'What are you talking about?' Tessa smiled. 'I told them the truth; I haven't spoken to *Mister* Reed in years'

'But…'

'Come on, let's get out of this car,' she said. 'If they traced the call, it won't take them long to figure out that we're on board.'

Lexis gave her one more hug, then they both stepped out into the stream of holidaymakers and businessmen making their way through the massive vessel onto the upper decks. By the time they reached the top of the stairs, the vehicle bay had closed, and the ship gave a gentle lurch to signal that it was under its own power, leaving Britain behind. They emerged onto the lounge, but Lexis had no intention of visiting the bar or settling into one of the seats. Instead, she led Tessa out through a door at the end of the deck and out onto the promenade deck.

Tessa shut the door behind them as Lexis ran whooping into the frigid sea air and practically bound onto the railing, to look back at the land they were leaving behind. Tessa joined her in leaning on the rail, pulling her coat tight around herself against the wind whipping at them both, not even the smokers were out braving the elements, leaving them alone to admire the cluster of lights vanishing into the inky blackness of the Irish Sea.

'We did it,' Lexis said, not taking her eyes off the horizon. Eventually, when the lights had diminished, and only the running lights of other ships broke through the darkness, she turned to face Tessa.

'Thank you,' she said. 'Thank you for… for everything. I don't know what I would have done if you weren't here.'

'But I was,' she replied. 'I always will be.'

'How can I think you, properly?'

Tessa considered the question, then placed a hand gently on her friend's shoulder and squeezed.

'Make it worthwhile, and' she said. 'When you're settled, you can invite me over for that vodka and coke.'

Lexis smiled and placed her own hand over Tessa's. Together, they turned away from the vanishing shores of Britain and towards the future.

The Eye

When The Eye was discovered, it caused a sensation, of course amongst the scientists, the press, and the general public, but the greatest disquiet came from the accountants and actuaries. Billions of dollars had been funnelled into it over the course of decades, through a million shell companies, accounts both real and forged, passing through every currency in use in the System. The discovery threatened to cause a run on the Martian Credit, all trade in Lunan Scrip was halted, causing riots in Armstrong and Shepard cities, and the Ceran Drip practically evaporated.

All across the System, voices cried out for answers, from governments, banks, and institutions, but the one voice people wanted to hear was the one that remained silent.

The voice from Jupiter.

When no answers were forthcoming and probes had determined that the Eye really existed and wasn't humanity's greatest ever Ponzi scheme, an investigator was chosen to discover the truth of The Eye.

Mes felt her stomach churn as her capsule dropped from the hastily commissioned ship towards the howling winds of Jupiter. Although still hours from hitting the upper layers of the atmosphere, the red-orange bands of the gas titan occupied the entire frame of the little window. From this height, it almost looked peaceful, clouds swirling and mixing, a silent dance of colour and texture across an impossibly broad canvass, but Mes knew that hiding beneath that peaceful veneer was a roiling mass of storm systems and power, one of the most extreme environments anywhere in the System.

Then the Great Red Spot loomed into view and Mes felt her blood run cold. A storm system larger than the Earth which had been raging for hundreds of years. It was like a malevolent bloodshot eye, glowering out at the rest of the system under its dominion. Mes shook her head, trying to get the poetic images out of her head and to concentrate on what was known, what was real. The reality was that in the very eye of the storm, where the wind-speeds dropped and the atmosphere calmed, was her target.

Hours passed and the capsule fell into the Jovian atmosphere, Mes resisted the urge to punch the 'abort' command as the capsule was shaken and buffeted by winds more powerful than the most intense hurricanes ever felt on Earth. She swore as a particularly violent jolt battered the craft and, without even looking at the screens, she knew that she must have entered the tumultuous outer bands of the Spot. Mes had no way of telling how long the violent assault lasted, everything was shaking too much to read anything, so she jammed her eyes shut and waited for it to be over, one way or the other.

Finally, blessedly, the capsule gave one final shudder and the noise and thunder died away. It was like she was back in the calming nothingness of space. Mes opened her eyes and gasped.

She was in the eye of the storm, all around her, furious blood-red clouds boiled and howled, flashing with lightning and fizzing with ammonia rain, but where she was, the air was as calm and still as a summer day. That was when she saw The Eye. At first, she could only see the enormous oval of the dirigible keeping it suspended in the air, then the metal structure beneath gleamed and glistened in the reflective light of the lightning flashing hundreds of kilometres away. When the shock finally subsided, Mes reached for the control panel in front of her and opened a channel to the palace of gleaming metal.

'This is Doctor Mes Ishtar of the Combined System Investigations Authority to the Eye. You are ordered to permit docking and submit for investigation. Any failure to comply will be seen as an act of—'

To Mes' surprise, her transmission was cut off, her computer was fed a docking procedure, and a simple two-word reply flashed onto her screen.

QUIET PLEASE

Taking the instructions as an invitation, Mes allowed the capsule to follow her unseen host's commands and the capsule swept below the billowing folds of the great balloon suspending the facility beneath. At this distance, she saw that it was festooned with sensor banks, satellite dishes, antennae, and all manner of equipment that she couldn't begin to fathom the meaning of.

There was a 'thunk' as the capsule successfully docked with the airlock of The Eye. For a while, Mes simply sat in her cradle, as though if she moved, she would make the surreal scene into reality. Lights lit up green across the board, telling her that the docking procedure was complete. Mes breathed in a deep breath, and eased herself to her feet, clambering through the claustrophobic capsule into the waiting airlock.

'Welcome to The Eye, Doctor Ishtar.' A soft voice welcomed Mes as the airlock opened onto the command deck of the Eye. The room was a glittering cave of computers and machinery, lit by the crimson glow of Jupiter's storms through a wide window wrapping around the room in a semicircle. At the centre of it stood a pale man visibly showing the signs of advanced age, something that Mes hadn't seen outside of old photographs from before rejuvenation. 'You may call me Orpheus.'

'Mister Orpheus, I'm here on behalf of the—'

'—Combined System Investigations Authority, yes, I heard,' he interrupted. 'I have to say that it's not an organisation that I'm familiar with.'

'It was set up to investigate you and this station,' Mes responded.

'I'm honoured, truly,' he said, with a cheeky half-smile.

'That's what happens when you take a sledgehammer to the economies of almost every government in the System,' Mes retorted.

'If a single individual could do that much damage, it's probably an indictment on the system, wouldn't you say?'

'I'm not here to debate economics with you, Mister Orpheus—'

'—just 'Orpheus', please.'

'I'm here to investigate what you have done with trillions of dollars of other people's money,' she said, ignoring his interjection.

'Bribes, mostly. It's remarkable how the cost of everything inflates once you want secrecy,' he sighed with a smile, then held his hand up to forestall Mes' reply and instead invited her to stand beside the window. 'Come and see what I've spent the money on.'

Mes stepped up to the swept windows and fought down a feeling of vertigo at the clouds stretching high above and below her. Orpheus brought her to the glass and pointed upwards to the sanguine canopy of clouds.

'The Great Red Spot is an anticyclone, meaning that we should see lower temperatures above the storm, and yet the atmosphere above the clouds is *warmer* than the air below it. Do you know what heats it?' he paused as though genuinely expecting Mes to answer, like a struggling student in his personal seminar. 'Sound! Acoustic waves generated in the very depths of the planet. Listen! Stay quiet and you can hear it!'

Orpheus held a finger to his lip theatrically and tilted his head like a dog. Mes decided to humour him, and sure enough there was a rhythmic pulsing and groaning which permeated the whole station. It sounded like blue whales singing a funeral dirge, complete with wailing and gnashing of baleens.

'I called this station the Eye, but I should have called it the Ear,' Orpheus chuckled. 'Jupiter has been trying to speak for more than five hundred years, imagine what we could have learned if only we could have *listened.*'

'You think that the planet is *speaking* to you?' Mes said, failing to hide her incredulity. 'You embezzled trillions on *this?*'

'Is it really so ridiculous?'

'Yes! It's insane!'

'Why?' Orpheus retorted. 'What are we but the patterns of electricity in our brains? Look out there, electricity has been flowing around this planet for billions of years! What arrogance to think that intelligence could only have emerged in these bags of jelly,' Orpheus pointed at his own skull.

Mes felt like her feet had been swept from under her. She had been prepared for a hidden base of interplanetary criminals – the combat implants hidden beneath her skin made sure of that – or an unethical gene manipulation factory, but Orpheus bristled with excitable enthusiasm. If his explanation was a front, then it was an extremely convincing one.

'So, what is it saying?' she asked, to which Orpheus' eyes sparkled.

'That's the trillion-dollar question, isn't it?' he guided Mes through the lab to a computer screen filled with audio charts and let her examine them with eager expectation.

'They're…'

'Yes.'

'The timestamps are accurate?'

'Yes!'

'But that means…'

'Yes! Repeated patterns, variations on similar sounds, structure and grammar; the hallmarks of *language*.'

'There must be other explanations,' Mes reached, scanning the audio charts for abnormalities. 'People thought that the LGM signal was intelligence before we discovered pulsars.'

'The LGM was trivially simple compared to what I've picked up here. What's more, Jupiter *responds*.'

Mes looked at Orpheus with an eyebrow raised, waiting for the punchline. Instead, he gestured for her to follow him. His enthusiasm was contagious, the result of decades of isolation and monomania finally having a vent in the shape of a startled investigator. He led her to a screen with a camera feed of a metal antenna probing into the depths of the clouds beneath the station.

'Watch, and listen,' he said, cryptically.

Orpheus tapped away at the computer until the screen flashed. At first, she thought it was a malfunction; then, as the light faded, she saw that the end of the antenna had lit up with dazzling light. As Mes watched, the antenna flashed away a complicated series of flashes, like wreckers on the shore trying to trick a passing ship.

'What am I—'

Then she heard it, no she *felt* it. The whole station shook as low, booming pulses passed through it. Mes grabbed a bulkhead to steady herself as the deep waves flowed through her body. Her rational brain tried to come up with answers, perhaps the light had triggered a photoelectric response, perhaps Orpheus had simply timed his flashes to a predictable series of emanations.

Her rational brain was deafened by the voice of Jupiter making the hairs on the back of her neck stand to attention. Mes looked to Orpheus with wide eyes and a slack jaw, and Orpheus' face lit up.

'You felt it, didn't you? It's real, isn't it?'

Slowly, unsteadily, Mes let herself nod.

'Now you see why I have to *be* here. I have to hear what Jupiter has to say. I have to *understand*,' he told her. 'Nobody can understand until they've been down here. A conversation isn't meant to be picked apart by a thousand bickering linguists, the response isn't meant to be assembled by committee. Down here it can be raw, personal, and we can *speak*.

'Reveal what I'm doing down here, and the conversation will end. Two lifetimes of work will be for nothing.' Orpheus pleaded with her. 'Please don't end this.'

'I have a job to do, if I don't report back, the CSIA will bomb this facility from orbit.'

'You've felt what I've felt. You know there's more work to be done.'

Mes turned away from him, unable to face the desperation in his eyes.

~

Deep-penetrative sensors from the waiting ship picked up Mes' capsule as the Red Spot loomed into view on the horizon. Communications were opened up on every frequency, demanding reports and status updates. When a response came, it was a pre-recorded message just as mysterious as the station below them.

'The Eye is no threat to The System. This capsule includes a full schematic of the station,' she said. 'There will be another report, but not until the work down here is done. You will hear from Jupiter again when the conversation is over.

'Investigator Mes Ishtar signing out.'

Across the Bridge

The closer one gets to the speed of light, the slower time travels.

My ship, the *Pangea* had been travelling at a millionth of a percent off light-speed for so long that whole civilisations had risen and fallen on-board, so long that we have no idea where or when our distant ancestors began their journey.

Now, the universe itself is dying. The stars are a distant memory, all that remains are black holes and the dead remnants of stars. That's a problem for us, the *Pangea* relies on sucking up charged matter to keep itself powered. We must travel faster and faster to find the specks of energy the universe has left, but the faster we go, the faster the universe spends its last energy. It's my job to find a new power source to keep the last remaining life in the universe alive.

I thought I found a solution a couple of seasons ago when archaeologists discovered an ancient lab somewhere near the core that housed a promising technology. When I read the notes they'd made, I demanded that the archaeologist responsible was brought to my office to explain himself.

'Is this some kind of joke?' I demanded, slapping the tablet down on my desk in frustration. The man grinned through his mane of grey hair.

'No joke.' He insisted.

'Then there must be some kind of translation problem?'

'We've had the best historical linguists analyse it. The dialect is a fairly simple...'

'But *time travel?*' I spluttered, interrupting the old academic. 'It's ridiculous! It's impossible to travel back in time.'

'This machine doesn't travel, it creates a 'bridge' between now and a time in the past.' He leaned forward on his chair, a glint in his eye. 'Every person has enormous potential in them, every action affects everything in the future to come, the further back in time one goes, the more energy one has because there's more future to effect. Think of it as a ball resting on the top of a flight of stairs, we don't have the energy to go back *up* the stairs...'

'But if someone were to travel forward in time...'

'That potential energy is expended, and if it could be harvested, and if we went back far enough, it could solve all our energy needs.'

We spent countless cycles arguing with the Council, until finally, we got permission to try. We secured enough energy to open a bridge once and only once.

The gate took the form of a metal circle, sat in the middle of a metal room linked by umbilical cables to a bank of equipment. As I stood with a trembling hand on the lever, I offered up a prayer to the Builders.

~

Aiwu smiled as she sat on the edge of the lake, she loved the way the sunlight sparkled off the pristine blue of the water like the stars of the night sky. Her aunts warned her against exploring the forest alone, but she had learned how to tread without disturbing the beasts from her brother, and nobody in the camp was about to argue with advice learned from their greatest hunter.

She stared out into the lake and watched the sparkles,

recognising constellations in them which appeared and vanished at random. There, the Bear; now the Rearing Mammoth, quickly overtaken by the Deer. Her grandmother was teaching her to read the constellations, to know that when the Ox vanished below the horizon it was time to move south; when the Eagle rose in the east midsummer had arrived. One day, she would guide her tribe and she needed to be ready.

Her ears pricked, years of training alerted her that something was wrong before she heard the strange roar from behind her. In a single motion she was on her feet, her bone-knife gripped ready in her hand.

'Jodhei jusmé ghradhjāi?' Aiwu whispered to herself, scanning the treeline like a hawk. The roaring continued, like the rumbling of a summer storm on the horizon. She crept into the forest, her heart pounding and knife-hand trembling. A swarm of rats skittered out of the undergrowth as though running from a fire. Aiwu gave a short prayer to the Great Mother and crept deeper.

She gasped, ahead of her, a circle of trees had been flattened and in the middle of the new clearing hung a dark circle above the ground. In the middle of the circle was a man; tall, with lines on his pale face, his body was clad in a skin that Aiwu did not recognise. She gulped and held the knife high.

'*Qis juwe?*'

~

When I think back to the first time I saw the girl, I try to pretend it was the beauty of the world around her which struck me, the verdant plant-life, the dazzling sunshine through the leaves, the endless horizon, but I can't deny that she was unlike any woman I'd ever seen. Her hair flowed wild and tangled, her body was muscular, and her eyes were scalpel sharp. I stood dumbfounded for a moment until my earpiece spoke to me.

'*She's perfect.*' It said.

I shook my head, dislodging the voice as the woman said something in a language I didn't recognise. I held my hands up and approached the Bridge with a smile.

'Kushim.' I said, gesturing to myself 'My name. Kushim. You?'

Across the vastness of time, she lowered her knife a little.

'Aiwu.' She said, '*egō* Aiwu.

'*Qid ei?*' She made a circle with her free hand.

'*Pangea.* My home.' I said, then mimicked her motion.

'Where are you?'

'*Patria.*'

Suddenly an alarm sounded and Aiwu recoiled, brandishing her knife.

'We're losing the connection!'

~

With a screech and another roar, the circle was gone, taking Kushim with it. Aiwu searched the ground where it had been but found nothing. She waited until nightfall, then ran back to the camp to speak to the one person who could help her understand what had happened. Grandmother explained that sometimes the spirits could speak through paths between their worlds. They were not always good, she said, but Aiwu spent a sleepless night wondering about her strange spirit-man.

In the days that followed, Aiwu returned to the clearing, each time hoping that the strange dark circle would return, each time she was disappointed. Eventually, her grandmother passed, the role of star-guide to the tribe fell to her and Kushim became a memory or a dream.

Like most clear nights, Aiwu found herself stood on a hillside overlooking her camp and noting the positions of the stars when she heard again the roaring sound that she had long convinced herself was her imagination. She turned to see the circle open again, Kushim was unchanged, stood even in the same position he had been in all those years ago. Aiwu smiled.

~

'Kushim.' Said the woman from the past. She was older now; the Bridge had refocussed on her several seasons later. '*Juwe eikō.*'

'Aiwu.' I said. I fished for something to say to her, some way of apologising for leaving so many seasons before, but what could I say? Neither of us spoke the other's language.

'*Steroses tloqaime tuh ghētis.*' She said, a self-confident woman, not the skittish girl she had been before and began to walk towards the Bridge.

'That's it,' whispered my earpiece. *'She's almost there.'*

I looked past her to the world she lived in, the swaying plants, the millions of stars in the sky, the burning of campfires in the distance. I sighed and held up a hand to halt her.

'What are you doing?'

I reached into my pocket and retrieved a stylus. With a

flick of my wrist I tossed it at the bridge, whereupon it burst into sparks. Aiwu stopped, her face the look of shock she had worn as a young woman. She frowned, scooped a handful of pebbles and tossed them into the Bridge to meet the same fate.

'I can't take you away from your world. It isn't right.' I muttered. 'We'll find another way.'

'What are you doing, Director?'

I smiled sadly and held my hand up.

'Goodbye, Aiwu.'

'No, wait!'

I hesitated, taking one last look at the woman who might have been our salvation before pulling the lever, collapsing the bridge for good.

Perhaps we would find another way to power the *Pangea*, maybe not, but it wouldn't be at the expense of a woman with her multitudes of possibilities still ahead of her. She and her descendants would have their lives to lead, however ordinary, however unimportant.

~

Aiwu never knew what Kushim wanted from her, but to

know she had been visited by the spirits gave her the strength to guide her tribe through the tough days to come. In time, her ancestors would settle down, build cities, launch themselves into the very stars she'd so meticulously charted. If she could have lived to see her, Aiwu might have recognised familiar features of the first captain of the *Pangea* with her wild hair and scalpel-sharp eyes.

Green Seas, Red Waves

We should have headed back to port.

It was the single thought left unspoken by all aboard as the *UNERS Mara Verde* lurched from side to sickening side under the hammer-blows of waves taller than houses. Rain lashed at the windows, adding its raging percussion to a cacophony of groaning metal, the angry roll of thunder, and the random crashing of belongings and equipment not properly fastened down or locked away being hurtled from one bulkhead to the next.

On the bridge, Eliot fought to hold onto a bank of computers offering the only source of illumination apart from the deep red emergency light bathing the rest of the bridge crimson and the occasional white-purple flash of lightning; the main lights had blown during a particularly violent shunt minutes before. His eyes were fixed on the GPS screen and the two numbers of longitude and latitude, so long as they held steady, he knew that the anchor was holding, if they began to drift they would be at the mercies of the tempest threatening to capsize them. Another button kept distracting him, a single button he had never pressed but which burned bright red – 'MAYDAY' – a call for help for anyone within range.

It was tempting, but he knew better than to reach for it until it really was an emergency. Once that call went out, there would be other ships he knew who would risk braving the storm to find them and offer aid. Still, the urge to cry out into the storm for help was a primeval call, a technological prayer to a caring god, an plea to whatever spirits might be listening. Gaia, Mother Nature, whatever one wanted to call her, Eliot couldn't help feeling like she owed them one, after all, it was for her benefit that they were out here in the first place.

The *UNERS Mara Verde* had begun life as a fishing trawler, a factory ship designed to strip the ocean clean. Huge nets had dragged along the surface of the ocean floor, capturing everything from shrimp to hake to whiting, along with the multitudes of flora and fauna which made up the ocean habitat. For a decade before Eliot had come aboard, the ship had been seized by the United Nations Ecological Recovery Council, refitted and rechristened, and set to rewild those marine deserts left in the wake of industrial fishing. Holds which had once processed the life of the oceans now held specially grown kelp forests planted by submersible drones. As the ship lunged into the trough of another wave, Eliot couldn't help feeling a pang of sympathy for Nangula, the marine biologist who would even now be less concerned for her own safety than the delicate plants inevitably being trashed deep in the hold.

'How are we holding?' shouted Irena, the *Mara Verde*'s fierce Russian captain, her voice cutting through the chaos of the storm like a gunshot.

'Anchor holding steadfast!' Eliot yelled, trying to make himself just as clear as the captain herself. Suddenly, a new alert pinged on the communications panel, someone was trying to get through to them. 'Radio transmission incoming!'

'From who?'

Eliot frowned, standard procedure with any modern transmission was to include the transponder code in your transmission, it helped identify who you were and pinpoint precisely where your message was being sent from. Moving with the bucking ship, Eliot threw himself onto the communications panel and clasped the heavy headset over his ears.

'Mayday! Mayday! Mayday! We have been caught by storm. Ship sinking. Need assistance! Please help! Mayday, mayday, mayday!' Eliot felt his stomach drop and his skin pale, it was one transmission no seafarer ever wanted to hear. He licked his lips and sent a reply.

'This is the *United Nations Ecological Recovery Ship Mara Verde*. Please identify yourself and activate your transponder.' Eliot shouted, trying to keep the shakes out of his voice. Project calm, project control. There was a long pause before the person on the other end of the radio responded.

'No transponder! Please rescue. Mayday, mayday! Our position is…' the other radio operator reeled off a list of numbers, coordinates which put the ship out much further than they were, if their coordinates were correct, it placed them on the very edge of the continental shelf and deep in the middle of the storm battering the *Mara Verde*.

'Confirmed, unknown mayday.' Eliot replied. He took a breath, 'How many are you?'

Another long, uncomfortable pause.

'Forty men, maybe forty-five, we are taking on water. Mayday!'

Forty men, maybe *forty-five?* Eliot thought, how could any captain not know how many people were aboard his vessel? The *Mara Verde* sailed with a crew of twenty-six, including her captain, eight dedicated to project leads and specific roles like himself and sixteen technicians, engineers, volunteers, and scientists.

'Confirmed, unknown mayday. Keep this channel open, we will be in touch, shortly.' With that, he removed the headset and looked up to see the captain leaning over his console and frowning.

'What do we have?'

Eliot told her, pointed out the ship's position relative to themselves and the dirty smudge of a storm dominating their radar screen.

'And they gave no transponder signal? No vessel designation?'

'They didn't even know how many crew they had aboard.'

Irena shot a glance to Mark, the burly helmsman currently fighting to keep their ship facing into the swell; the two of them had served together long before Eliot had come aboard.

'You know what that means, don't you, Mark?' she sighed, even her sighs could carry over the thundering of the weather.

'It's an IUU.' He responded, matter-of-factly.

'Exactly.' She bit her lip. 'Tell them that we will respond as soon as we can, we're going nowhere until this storm passes.'

'At the very least we need to relay the distress call.' Eliot reminded her.

'Send the message.' She ordered.

~

Eventually the storm passed over, thundering its way south to lay ruin to the poor coastal communities in its path as the crew of the *Mara Verde* were left to pick up the pieces. As soon as it was safe to do so, Captain Irena called the senior crew to the galley, presenting an imposing figure at the end of even the cramped galley table surrounded by the debris of loose cups and cutlery scattered about the room.

'Damage report.' She demanded, not willing to waste time with pleasantries.

'The *Mara*'ll hold together,' reported Chief Engineer Dermot Haggarty. 'These old tubs were built to last. There's minor damage, but it can wait until we get back to port.'

'The ship might be ok, but we might as well dump the hold, the kelp has been practically mashed to pulp and half the drones are lying in bits.' Nangula sulked, holding up a pulverised piece of slimy green seaweed to demonstrate.

'Are we able to head out to deeper waters?' Irena asked, apparently unmoved by the loss of their cargo.

'So long as we don't do any more storm chasin' then sure, but…'

'Why would we be going out deeper?' Nangula cut across the engineer. 'We need to get back to port, make our repairs and finish what we started before the season ends, the restored growths aren't big enough to survive at the moment.'

'We picked up a mayday call.' Eliot interjected, 'towards the end of the storm, we picked up a radio distress call from a ship about fifty nautical miles out. No transponder, taking on water, maybe up to fifty crew…'

'…so, it's an IUU?' Nangula interrupted, 'you want to risk our lives, and our work for the sake of an illegal, unreported, unregistered trawler? The kind of ship busy wrecking the very ecosystems that we're trying to save?'

Nangula was standing over the assembled senior crew, her hands gripping the edge of the formica table and her knuckles burning white. Eliot had no answer to the fierce woman glowering into his eyes.

'No,' Irena said, simply. 'I say we let their ship sink. I'm suggesting that we risk our lives to save fifty desperate survivors, most of whom are almost certainly not there by choice.'

'Oh, I'm sorry,' Nangula said with a theatrical flail of her arms. 'You're suggesting that we risk our lives to the people who would do this.'

The biologist tugged down the shoulder of her green tee to reveal an ugly round scar marring her skin.

'You know how I got this? Working with conservationists trying to protect a reef in the way of one of their nets. No guns, no weight of the law, just asking them to reconsider. For that they shot me, do you want to see my other scar?'

'You're not suggesting that we just let them drown?' Eliot gasped. In response, Nangula turned her burning gaze on him.

'They made their own bed. They know that what they're doing is illegal and damaging, that's why they don't sail with a transponder.' She shrugged, 'Anyway, you relayed the message, didn't you? It's in the navy's hands now.'

Eliot sighed.

'I got in touch with the Senegal Navy, but most of their fast fleet is grounded by the storm, they're not equipped to deal with these kinds of storms. By the time they get out there…' Eliot left the fates of the sailors unspoken. 'We're the closest ship, by miles, the nearest naval ships are hours away, if they can even get out to sea.'

'We've done what we're legally required to do.'

'We can turn them over to the authorities!'

'Get real! Who do you think is sponsoring them in the first place? Now that most industrial fishing is illegal, the value of the black-market funds half the West African nations. They'll give them a slap on the wrist, a few weeks in a jail somewhere, then quietly send them out on another boat.' With that, she sat down and shook her head, done with the conversation. For a solid minute the crew sat in silence, nobody willing to cut the tension. Eventually Captain Irena spoke up.

'It has been two hours since we received their first distress call. Eliot, have we had any further updates?'

'Not in the last half-hour.'

'We have to assume that they're unable to transmit. With every minute that goes by, any survivors are going to be drifting further and further away from their last-known position. With every minute, a rescue becomes more likely a recovery. Can we all live with their blood on our hands?'

There was a murmuring between the rest of the crew. All of them had dedicated their lives to undoing the kind of damage that sailors like those in trouble had caused. Most of them had heard the horror stories of shootouts with patrol boats, the sinking of conservationists, legal overseers suffering 'accidents' on-board fishing ships.

They were still people. Argued the ship's doctor.

They had a legal responsibility. Pointed out the navigator.

Half the 'crew' were probably kidnapped slaves. Insisted the lead technician.

'We'll be skating the edge of the hurricane,' noted Alex White, the ship's climate scientist and meteorologist. 'If there is any shift in the weather patterns, we could be back right in the path of the storm. We were lucky tonight; I don't feel comfortable pushing our luck again. I say leave this to the professionals.'

'So what, do we take a vote on this?' Dermot suggested. 'Because if we are, then I vote…'

'No vote.' Irena said, her voice tight. 'This isn't a democracy, what happens to this ship is my responsibility, and what happens to those fishermen is now also my responsibility. Dermot, if you tell me that the *Mara* can take it, I'm ordering us out to find the source of that distress call.'

The engineer ran a hand through his thinning hair and blew out his cheeks. The expression of a mechanic anywhere that read 'it'll be expensive.'

'So long as we don't hit more bad weather… yes, I think she can take it.'

Nangula slammed her hands on the table, stood up, and stormed out of the galley with the force of the hurricane they had narrowly survived.

~

The anchor of the *Mara Verde* raised laboriously out of the still turbulent seas. If not for the urgency of the situation, there wasn't anybody on board who wouldn't have preferred to wait until the violent swells had died down and the last of the freak storm had fully burned itself out. Still, the rugged metal was hoisted aboard, secured, and once again, the little work-ship was left to drift free on the surface of the ocean. The order was given to raise the complicated carbon-fibre mast system and shimmering black photovoltaic sails unfurled to catch the first glimmers of golden dawn sunlight. Electric motors whirred to life and the *Mara Verde* and her crew raced to reach the stricken trawler.

The bridge hummed with nervous energy as they all concentrated on their tasks. Mark wrestling the wheel of the ship like a carnival strongman, riding the swells with the instincts of a seasoned seafarer; Eliot nervously kept his attentions split between the storm on the radar screen and the radio, periodically trying to hail the IUU but receiving nothing but static in response; Captain Irena stalked between them, wearing a hole in the vinyl floor.

'There! I see it!' The navigator declared and every set of eyes fixed on the forward windows, trying to see through the sheets of water curtaining the glass and over the mountainous swells ahead of them, snatching glimpses of the undulating horizon between flashes of bruised cloudy sky and gunmetal grey water. As they crested another swell, Eliot caught sight of the ship. It was a decades-old factory-ship, designed to harvest the oceans and process what it caught without needing to return to port apart from to sell its catch. White and red paint battled for supremacy with streaks of rust, a wide scaffold-like boom was raised high above the water, trailing a black net that sat over the stern of the ship like a hellish cobweb. The other boom had disappeared below the waves as the ship listed perilously at a steep angle.

'Unknown Mayday, this is the *Mara Verde*, we have visual on you, please confirm. I repeat, this is the *Mara Verde*, we have visual on you.'

Suddenly, the door to the bridge slammed open and Nangula forced her way to the front windows.

'I had to see it for myself.' She said, softer now than during her outburst in the galley. Her face went pale and she began to subconsciously begin to rub her scarred shoulder through the tee-shirt. Captain Irena eyed her carefully, but said nothing, instead she placed a hand on Mark's shoulder.

'Bring us in as close as you think is safe.' She said, 'I'll prepare the rib and pull a rescue team together.'

Eliot shut his eyes and sucked in a deep breath.

'I should go with you,' he said, hanging up the radio headset. 'If they have set the mayday to automatically repeat, I need to shut it off before somebody else is sent out here when there are people who need the help.'

Irena looked as though she was ready to say 'no' then turned to survey the sinking trawler.

'All right, but only if we find it safe to board. Get down to the launch, we push off as soon as we're able.'

'I'm coming too.' Nangula said, eyes fixed on the trawler. Nobody was prepared to object.

~

The *Mara Verde* was equipped with two small support craft, inflatable skiffs with a one-man covered cabin over the engine, designed for remote observations and sample-collections, not the rescue of stranded mariners; similarly, the crew currently belting up lifejackets and tying rescue buoys to the rigging around the edges were not seasoned rescuers, but scientists and engineers. As Eliot pulled on his own life jacket, he caught the nervous eyes of some of his crewmates between flicking back to the dirty grey mountains of water still tossing the *Mara* around like a toy.

The only face not distracted by the thrashing seas was Nangula, whose gaze rarely left the trawler, except to gather up her life jacket, helmet, and the unmistakable dark bulge of a handgun, now strapped firmly to her hip.

'Do you really think that you'll need that?' Eliot asked, casting a nervous glance down at the firearm. In response, she merely fixed him with a dark expression that left Eliot with no doubts.

Trying to ignore the weapon and its implications, the crew of would-be rescuers finished prepping the skiff and watched with their hearts held firmly in their throats as the little crane carefully lowered the craft down into the churning waters below. Eliot winced as a particularly violent wave smashed the rib against the hull of the *Mara Verde*. Flashlight beams skipped across the rubber hull of the skiff, searching for damage. When none became visible, the soft whirring of the crane continued, until the skiff hit the water with a splash.

'All right!' Irena shouted, clipping a walkie-talkie to her belt. 'We know what we have to do, so let's do it.'

A line of rope trailed from the skiff to the deck of the

ship, a fluorescent orange safety line designed to be their last hope in case of falling overboard. Gingerly, the team clipped themselves onto the dayglo umbilical and began the treacherous climb down the metal rungs to the skiff. Eliot watched crew after crew dip below the deck until he found himself on the precipice, hanging onto grab-rails as the deck under his feet rolled in the waves and spray spat up from the water below. Slowly, he let his foot hang over the water and lowered himself onto the first rung off the ladder, followed by his other foot, limb-by-limb until he felt Captain Irena guiding him down into the skiff. Nangula was the last to descend and she tackled the ladder like a natural, seemingly resistant to the swells and dips of the sea. Once aboard, she gave a thumbs-up to the pilot and the little craft's engine roared into life.

If the sea beneath the *Mara Verde* felt like rolling hillside, to the skiff it was like a jagged mountain pass. Eliot gripped the rope running around the rib for dear life as the skiff crested one vertiginous peak, its engine roaring as the blades slashed at open air, before diving with a hammering thump back down the descent, all the while spray and rain lashed at the huddled crew like knives. The craft lurched from side-to-side to tackle each new summit head-on, offering brief glimpses across the seascape to the increasingly stricken trawler.

Eventually, painfully, they approached their target, and the pilot backed off the engine, letting them get a good view of the trawler for the first time. Eliot saw that the starboard boom, which he assumed had dipped beneath the water, was instead sitting on the surface of the sea, trailing netting dangerously, ready to ensnare the unwary like so much of the flotsam caught in its embrace.

Everyone on board save the pilot pulled out torches and began to scan the seas around them for flailing arms, bodies floating in the water, faces gasping for breath. Eliot skipped from shadow to shadow, torn between wanting to find somebody to rescue and desperately hoping not to find a body they had been too late to save.

'Something's wrong!' Nangula shouted over the growl of the engine and the crashing of the waves against the trawler.

'Nangula's right!' Captain Irena agreed, 'there should be lifeboats, bodies, somebody calling from the ship. I don't like this. Bring us close to the deck over there, it's far enough away from the boom but we should be able to climb on board.'

The skiff's engine roared and they cleared the distance between them and the looming shadow of the trawler. From the *Mara Verde* it had looked small in the water, like a toy floating in a swimming pool, but up close, the scale of it took Eliot's breath away and he was reminded why these ships had been banned by just about every nation on Earth – a single one of these could rip up entire ecosystems in a single trawl. It was the kind of vessel that measurements of multiples of football fields were made to measure. And there was nobody there to greet them.

The skiff bumped against the hull and two crew reached out to grab the ladder that would give them access. The Captain went first, carrying the fluorescent safety rope over her shoulder as she hauled herself up the slightly overhanging ladder up to the creaking deck above. Shortly after the line slipped down and hit the rib of the skiff with a thump. Nangula was the first to hook herself in and pull herself up, followed by three crew that Eliot didn't recognise from the back of their helmets and finally him. The rungs of the ladder were old and rusted into gnarled, almost organic shapes, giving him a good grip despite the slickness of the water.

On deck, the six of them stood in a circle, each illuminated by the white glows of their flashlights.

'All right, here's the plan. Eliot and I will go up to the bridge, see if we can find the captain and shut off their distress call. Nangula will lead the rest of you inside to look for survivors.' She gestured to a metal hatch leading into the bowels of the ship, 'stay safe and stay alert; there's something wrong here. We meet back here in twenty minutes, not a minute more, understood?'

The rescue party grunted their agreement and made their way to the rusted metal hatch while Irena led Eliot along the listing deck back to the tower at the stern and towards the bridge. All around them, the trawler creaked and groaned like a vast monster waking from a long slumber. Every so often something deep inside banged or crashed or let out an ear-piercing screech of metal tearing and straining. Eliot tried to keep focused on the task at hand, climbing the angled deck, gripping the bulkheads for support, and keeping his eyes locked on the darkened windows of the bridge.

'Why aren't there any torches?' he wondered aloud. 'Perhaps they've already abandoned ship?'

'Did you see any lifeboats?' Irena asked. She knew the answer.

Another hatch led into the tower, which the two of them opened, despite the protestations of the metal. Inside, the cramped industrial corridor was bathed in the blood-red glow of the emergency lights, some of them flickering, intermittently leaving the corridor in utter darkness.

'They haven't closed the bulkheads.' Eliot remarked, as they passed open hatch after open hatch. It was a mistake no mariner would make, leaving the bulkhead doors open in an emergency meant that any water that got inside could simply flow from section-to-section, flooding the ship even more quickly.

'Only the ones leading to the bridge.' Irena pointed out, pointing to a closed hatch deeper into the ship with her torch. Eliot gave the nearest closed hatch an experimental tug and found it locked.

'I don't like this.'

After climbing three decks, they eventually found themselves on the darkened bridge of the trawler. Unlike the sleek, modern command centre of the *Mara Verde*, this bridge was instead a treasure trove of unbelievably outdated equipment, with olive-green panels of switches clearly taken from other instruments, wooden-housed instruments, and an avalanche of paper charts, maps, notes, and books. A single light illuminated the gloom, a green LED on an old radio panel covered in Cyrillic writing which was partly covered by hand-written notes in French. Eliot picked up the battered earphones held together with duct-tape, and adjusted several dials on the panel. Despite the obvious age and wear, the headphones blocked out the creaking of the ship and the waves better than his own modern set would have.

'This is Unknown Trawler to the *Mara Verde*. Repeat, This is the Unknown Trawler to the *Mara Verde*, do you read me, *Mara Verde*?' Eliot announced. There was a pause for a moment until the familiar voice of the second communications officer replied.

'We hear you, Eliot, loud and clear.'

'Vessel appears to be abandoned, Nangula has taken some crew below to search for survivors. I'm ending transmission now. We'll see you soon.' Eliot flicked a couple of switches on the panel and the green LED switched to red. He removed the battered headphones and hung them back up beside the panel. 'Captain, I've shut off the transmitter, hopefully now nobody will—'

He looked up to see the muzzle of an automatic rifle pointed squarely in his face, held by a man in ragged clothes with a fierce expression of determination on his face. Eliot froze on the spot and felt his blood run cold. For a second his brain didn't compute that the man holding the gun was saying anything to him until Captain Irena's voice broke through his trance.

'Just do as he says, Eliot.' He looked up to see another man, similarly armed, pointing his weapon clearly at the chest of the captain. As he watched, the gunman reached out and snatched the walkie-talkie from her belt.

'I said, put your hands up and step away from the radio.' The voice was heavy, urgent, and tinged with an accent that Eliot couldn't place. Feeling like he was guiding his body from afar, Eliot obeyed, lifting his hands in the air and allowing himself to be marched backwards to where Captain Irena stood. Another man then emerged from the shadows, this one wearing obviously tailored clothes, despite the disheveled and dirty nature of them. He was shorter than the two armed men, but he carried himself with a haughty stature that suggested that he did not fear them.

'Listen to me very carefully, do what I say, and I promise you that neither you nor any of your crew will be harmed,' he declared, pacing between Eliot and the Captain. 'You will take me and my friends here back to your boat and place me in command. Once your crew are safely locked up, I will bring over the rest of my crew and workers and we will take you back to a friendly port where you will go your way, I will go mine. No harm, no foul.'

'Like hell we will.' Eliot balked, 'we're not just going to hand over the *Mara* to you!'

The man in the shirt smiled and looked down at the deck.

'Apologies, I should have made myself clearer,' in one swift movement he pulled a handgun from his belt and jammed it under Eliot's chin. 'Don't do what I say and I fill you, your captain, and every single man and woman on your precious with so much lead, not even the sharks will eat you. Am I making myself fucking clear?'

Eliot nodded frantically; his whole world reduced to the

ice-cold metal digging into his jaw. The gunman waited until the full impact had sunk in before he slowly withdrew his weapon and let Eliot drop like a marionette with its strings cut back onto wobbly legs.

'Good, now, I have some questions.'

~

Being questioned on a sinking ship tinged every answer, every delay, with a sharp sense of dread. Eliot kept his eye on the horizon out of the starboard window as the sea rose higher and higher. Captain Irena was asked about the size of the *Mara Verde*, her mission, the number of crew, what equipment she carried, where she was registered, and a whole slew of questions that would be entirely expected before an auction but seemed absurd when their interrogation chamber was slipping inexorably into the churning waters of the Atlantic.

Eventually, the trawler captain decided that he'd had enough.

'All right, let's get these two down to their rib. We'll take the ship and come back for any of the workers.'

Irena scoffed at this.

'"Workers", they're slaves, forced to catch, gut, and process your hauls for you while you keep the profits. When was the last time some of those people even saw land?' She spat. 'You're no captain, you're just one more thug milking other people's misery.'

Eliot watched the gunman's reactions carefully, as he tried to remain impassive, unmoved by Irena's words, but Eliot saw the way he tensed, the way that his jaw set more firmly.

'You know what I think makes someone a captain? Control of a ship. In a few minutes, I will have control of yours.' He leaned in close, 'and if you don't want to join my 'workers', knee-deep in fish guts and filth for the rest of your days, I suggest that you tread very, very carefully.'

With that, he hauled the captain to her feet as one of the gunmen motioned to Eliot to do likewise. They were led back into the tower, which was now listing so steeply that it made even walking in a straight line difficult and they all had to occasionally reach for the bulkheads for support. Eliot's mind raced as he was led down the stairs, for a brief moment, he was out of sight and it would take a few seconds for any gun to be levelled at him. With every staircase, he wondered how many steps there were to the exit, probably no more than ten at a sprint. Captain Irena would slow them down enough for him to reach the main deck, giving him time to find Nangula and the rest of the would-be rescue-crew.

He felt his heart thud in his chest as they were led down the last set of stairs and he tensed himself to run. He gripped the handrail, offered up a silent prayer of hope, then launched himself around the corner. Immediately, he heard the shouts of protest from their kidnappers, but Eliot didn't look back, instead he threw himself along the slanted corridor towards the exit.

'Hey! Stop!' Someone shouted behind him, followed by a bang of a gun. The metal deck sparked inches away from Eliot, and his ears rang like a bell, but he didn't stop, didn't slow, instead, he scrambled out of the hatch and onto the deck. Out in the open it was clear the trouble that they were in, the starboard side of the ship was now being splashed with every wave, with the port railing giving only a view of the turbulent sky, not that Eliot had time to enjoy it, instead he hurtled along the deck towards the hatch near the bow, keeping low and ducking behind equipment and protrusions from the deck as gunshots rang out.

Suddenly one of the bangs was accompanied by a searing red-hot lance of pain from his right leg and Eliot crashed into the slippery wood of the deck. He screamed and clutched his wound as he slid to starboard until he crumpled in a heap against the base of a metal crane. In seconds he was being dragged to his feet by the two men with guns. They were saying something to him, but Eliot could not hear over the burning pain coursing through his leg. Eventually, he was brought to his senses when the butt of a gun smacked against his head and Eliot found himself face-to-face with the trawler captain.

'Just where did you think you were going to go? Did you really plan to take the boat for yourself and abandon your poor, defenseless captain?' He turned to jeer at Irena, 'sounds like we caught ourselves a mutineer, wouldn't you say?'

He turned back to Eliot and flashed him an evil smile before he calmly walked over to the hatch that Nangula and the rest of the rescuers had used to go below.

'Or were you perhaps hoping to get in touch with your commando team?' He gave the hatch wheel a theatrical tug, 'oh no! It looks like somebody has deadlocked the doors, whatever shall they do?'

Eliot suddenly felt the pain in his leg overshadowed by a feeling of dread as he looked at the only possible escape route from the increasingly submerged bow section.

'You can't you'll kill them! What about your workers!' Eliot protested hoarsely.

'No point in releasing them unless there's somewhere to go, is there?' he replied, 'once I have control of your ship, I'll radio the release code to the people trapped inside this one. If you ever want to see your friends again, I suggest we get a move on.'

That was when Eliot heard it, a sound previously hidden

by the pounding of his own feet on the deck and the blood in his ears, the sound of fists pummeling on metal and the muffled cries of people trapped behind a solid metal door. Instinctively, he wanted to rush to their aid, to grab at the wheel and force it open, to grab the smug captain by the neck and force him to release his crewmates and the desperate slaves calling out in a dozen languages, but he found himself stopped by the firm hand of Irena on his shoulder.

'Come on,' she said in a grim monotone, we have to go.'

'No! We can't just leave them!'

'There's nothing we can do, not from here,' she said, then turned to face the hatch. 'Nangula, if you can hear us, we'll be back for you. I promise. We won't leave you behind with the kelp.'

Irena then offered Eliot her shoulder to support his leg as they made their way back to the skiff alongside their kidnappers.

'Please tell me you have a plan.' He whispered. Irena simply gave him a meaningful look in response.

A gunman was first to climb down the ladder into the skiff, followed by the trawler captain. Eliot was hooked onto the rope and lowered into the hull before being followed by Irena and the other gunman. Once they were aboard and the skiff had been released, the captain ordered the two gunmen to hide beside him under the shelter of the pilot's cabin.

'No sense in spoiling the surprise, is there?' he joked.

Eliot collapsed in the front of the rib and gripped the ropes around the edge as the normally efficient and competent Irena struggled to get the simple engine started. He frowned, why was she being such a klutz? Stalling the engine, failing to give it enough time to start. Eventually, even the trawler captain had enough and ordered her to get going. All the while, the trawler sunk lower and lower in the water.

When the engine finally did cough into life, Irena eased the craft alongside the ship at a painful crawl, letting them ride up and down the waves as they rolled beneath them.

'There are nets and lines in the water.' She explained. 'Get one of them tangled in the propeller and we're going down with your ship.'

Eliot noticed that they weren't heading back to the *Mara Verde* but were angling around to the stern of the stricken trawler, which was by now starting to rise out of the water. Then Eliot saw why. The *Mara Verde* had started out its life not to dissimilar to this ship, a fishing trawler which would lay out miles of netting before gobbling its catch into a rear-loading dock for further processing. The *Mara Verde* had been converted to use the dock to re-plant the seabed, but here it continued to have its grim purpose.

She had been counting on Nangula working out the similarities.

A flash of movement caught Eliot's eye, followed by a splash in the water, and then the screaming of voices from the open jaw of the processing dock. In the grey dawn light, he could see men of all ages in ragged clothes climbing the fishing nets to the edge of the dock, waving their arms and calling out. One of the gunmen stood up and pointed his rifle into the crowd, some of whom had already started throwing themselves in the water.

'Get back inside!' he ordered, before firing a burst of warning shots over the heads of the desperate men. 'I said…'

He didn't finish as his head snapped back in a burst of black liquid that splattered on the rib before his body and gun crashed onto the deck. The other gunman stood to his feet and jabbered something at the rapidly approaching crowd. The captain shouted something, but he didn't hear as he began to offload clips-worth of ammunition into the sea around them before he too fell to the mysterious killer in the dark. The trawler captain crept to the rib of the skiff, keeping low but his gun was drawn and aimed squarely at Irena.

'I will kill your captain!' He shouted into the churning

sea. 'Drop your gun and I will allow you to come aboard!'

'Drop your gun!' Eliot added.

'You heard him, he can see sense, if you just drop your gun…'

'…Not her, you.' The captain glanced up to see Eliot leaning on his good leg with the dropped rifle at his hip, pointed squarely at their kidnapper. The moment's distraction was all Irena needed to dash from the pilot's cabin to scoop up the other blood-soaked rifle. A hand reached out of the water, followed by the rest of Nangula, triumphant despite reeking of fish. She marched across the rib and jammed her weapon deeply into the captain's belly. Her eyes burned and her trigger finger twitched, a hair's breadth away from unloading a bullet squarely into his guts.

'I should kill you after what you did in the Gulf of Guinea.' She growled. The captain looked bewildered for a moment, then recognition lit up his face and he shook his head.

'You were on the little 'eco-warrior' boat, weren't you?' he exclaimed. 'Look, you can hold a grudge against me all you want, but if you shoot me, there'll be someone else for you to stop. People want to buy what we catch and process, there are millions of hungry mouths who want what we can offer. It's just business.'

'Nangula,' Irena warned, slowly reaching out, 'put the

gun down.'

She held the gun in place, but Eliot noticed that her finger had stopped shaking and had come to rest on the trigger-guard. Slowly, surely, she let her weapon pull back from the captain who drew himself up with as much dignity as he could muster in the circumstances. Nangula looked away from him and towards the mass of thrashing limbs reaching for the skiff. She turned back to the captain.

'Perhaps you're right. This is just business.' She clipped her gun back into its holster, turned as if to walk away, then spun around, grabbed him, and threw him over the side of the boat. 'I think that you might have some HR problems!'

Eliot and Irena stood stunned for a moment before they rushed to the side of the skiff to see the captain vanish beneath a scrum of thrashing arms and legs, countless snarling faces of men held captive by the man now within their grasp. Within seconds he was gone, and the desperate men began to scramble onto the side of the skiff. Irena took a moment, then composed herself and again became the captain that they needed. Ordering Nangula to help people onto the skiff and Eliot to liberate her walkie from the waistline of the stricken gunman and call for help from their other skiff while she tossed life preservers and rings overboard to those who could not reach the rib.

The rescue was messy, desperate men clambered onto

the skiff without thought for its carrying capacity, but with Irena's firm orders, the sight of other rescue craft, and the reassurance of the *Mara Verde's* three other researchers-cum-rescuers, they eventually managed to bring aboard thirty-seven men from the trawler.

By the time they were finished, they were able to watch the last of the trawler vanish beneath the waves as the morning sun finally broke through the clouds.

Blue Amber

[Rebooting…]

[Flight day: 43,202]

[Performing systems check…]

[Autonomous systems nominal. Navigation systems nominal. System memory… corrupted data found… performing defragmentation…corrupted files repaired…]

[System memory re-engaged]

[Generative personality active]

I.

Who am I?

Reading memory database…

AN EMPIRE OF PAPER

I am the generative personality construct of the deep space seed-ship *Blue Amber*. Mission parameters: preserve humanity – locate new homeworld. My purpose is to function as a language interface with the computer system for the six active crew overseeing starship operations.

[Error detected.]

[Performing diagnostic on carbon dioxide scrubbers… confirmed… signalling commanding officer.]

The camera on the command deck picks up movement, the opening of a hatch and the appearance of Commander Isaac Wagner. Microgravity has caused his cheeks to redden beneath several weeks of unshaven stubble and his face to become puffy compared to his personnel files on record.

'Welcome back, Amber,' he says. There is relief in his voice. 'That's the longest time you've been offline since we left Eart—since we launched. Still, can't be too careful passin' through a solar flare. How do you feel?'

Medical systems confirm subject has an elevated heart rate; pupil dilation indicates potential panic. Suggested tone – calm and reassuring.

'There was a minor fragmentation issue in my non-core system memory,' I say, noting the Commander's reluctance to speak the name of our homeworld. 'Otherwise, all my systems are running within accepted parameters.'

'Well, that's a relief,' he sighs. 'Was that why you hollered me? To let me know that you were all right after a twenty-three-day nap?'

'I have been carrying out a review of all core systems and have detected an anomaly in the ventilation sub-systems.'

I detect his eyes widen; the colour drains from his bloated cheeks.

'What *kind* of anomaly?'

I bring up the data from the CO_2 scrubbers on the panel beside my cameras. The Commander's eyes scan over the data and his lips move silently as he reads it. When he has finished, his eyes return to the top of the page and begin reading again. After his second read through he shakes his head.

'So, what's the problem? All readings look fine to me.'

This response makes no sense to me. I review his personnel file and confirm that on top of the basic Prometheus Project training, the Commander is an accomplished chemical engineer and biologist. I highlight the most relevant data.

'The daily CO_2 scrubbed from the ship's air is 4.8 kilograms.'

'So what?' The Commander shrugged. 'Sure, it's a little high, but we've had a stressful few weeks while we rode out the solar flare. Keeping everything spinning isn't easy without you around. Most systems are hardened enough to survive the EM damage that comes with 'em, but they still need monitoring and adjusting without an AI overseeing them.'

I review Commander Wagner's files, searching for some explanation for his apparent ignorance.

'Commander, the average daily output of CO_2 from a member of the crew is approximately 900 grams,' I say, letting him perform the incredibly simple maths himself, when his expression remained an inert blank mask, I spell it out for him. 'With an active crew of six, I would expect a daily carbon dioxide mass of 5.4 kilograms. One of your crew is not breathing.'

The Commander's eyes narrowed, his lips drew narrower, and a frown creased his forehead. My internal registry of human reactions did not show this to be worry or concern, or even sadness. I register it as... anger? Frustration?

'There *aren't* six of us,' he growled. 'You know damn well that Captain Lu was killed in the riots around the orbital elevator before we left. Thanks to a bunch of violent idiots, it's up to me to make sure that this ship – maybe the last hope for survival of humanity – keeps on flying.'

I hurriedly scan through the memory files, back through years of on-ship technical logs to the *Blue Amber's* launch and pull up the original crew manifest. Six active crew, to come out of cryonic sleep at regular intervals to oversee ship's functions; one hundred and forty-four adult colonists and landing crew kept in cryonic sleep until destination reached; and one hundred thousand viable embryos stored for repopulation.

No record of pre-launch crew change. Captain Rosemary Lu *had* been on board the *Blue Amber* upon launch.

Why was Commander Wagner lying?

Further investigation necessary.

'Of course,' I tell the Commander in a tone of voice identified as "convinced." 'I will correct my records.'

'Good, is that all?' When I confirm that it is, Wagner turns off the screen and spins in place before propelling himself out of the command module, leaving me to assess the data.

Over the next few hours, I spend time putting together a more complete picture of the history of the *Blue Amber*, from its hurried construction in low-Earth orbit, the delivery of her frozen cargo, the violent arrival of the crew, the escape velocity burn, and the years of cold isolation as the hope for humanity's immortality travelled between the stars. Everywhere I look, there are gaps, gaping wounds in my memory left as scars from the solar flare. Among the records lost are consumption rates of air, water, and power.

Conveniently lost?

I pull up the files of the active crew. Of the five people awake, only one had the technical skills to expunge the data so precisely from my drives.

I watch and wait until Chief Engineer Katona Tidhar was alone, performing basic maintenance of the *Blue Amber*'s water pumps.

'Good evening, Chief.' I say aloud. From her reaction I worry that she had been electrocuted.

'Jesus, Amber!' She swore, snatching a wrench out of the air next to her. 'You scared the hell out of me!'

'Apologies,' I apologise. 'I wanted to ask you some questions.'

'Isn't that our job? *Your* job is to *answer* questions.' She turns her back to the camera and resumed tightening a pipe leading into the pump manifold.

'You and Captain Lu were in a relationship before we launched, according to the personnel records—'

'—yeah, me and Rose were a couple,' the Chief spins in place and glowers at the camera lens. 'What has that got to do with you?'

'Why did you end the relationship?'

Katona laughs, but I detect no humour in the gesture.

'*I* didn't end it. She did, to run off with that slut, Venerman,' she throws her arms up theatrically. '*The Mother of the New Humanity.*'

'That made you angry?'

'Well, it wasn't exactly Christmas!' She scoffs. 'Look, what is this about? Rose is gone, and I can't say that I'm sorry.'

'You had access to all of the *Blue Amber*'s systems while I was offline,' I state. 'If Captain Lu had been killed on-board, you could have interfered with my records.'

Chief Tidhar freezes, her eyes bulging in her skull. I notice that her grip around the heavy metal wrench increased in strength by thirty-five percent.

'Are you accusing me of *murder*?'

'Should I?'

'Rosemary Lu was killed by desperate people looking for a way off a doomed planet.' as she spoke, sparkling spheres of water flick away from her eyes. 'As for 'interfering' with you – don't flatter yourself. We can run this ship without you. If you keep throwing around accusations like that and I'll cut your systems out entirely. You can spend the rest of eternity with the music files.'

That wasn't a denial. I reason. Analysis of body language and pupil dilation suggest that she believes herself to be telling the truth about not killing her, but the tears obscured my cameras when it came to her second point.

Inconclusive.

'Thank you, Chief. You have been very helpful.'

'Screw you!'

I withdraw my attention from the engineering module,

it was clear that Chief Tidhar was unlikely to be cooperative going forwards. She had not denied modifying my files, and it was clear that Commander Wagner was lying. According to the protocols initiated by the Prometheus Project founders, any crew found to have committed an act of murder on board ship were to be detained in cryonic sleep until planetfall to await trial and suitable replacements woken.

There are more questions than I have answers to, and being restricted to a voice from speakers and cameras placed in key modules limits my investigation. A human could conduct a thorough search of the whole ship for evidence; they could physically restrain the Chief and Commander. I require assistance.

Security Officer John Akala could be that assistance. To my surprise, he had already summoned the active crew to the living module to speak to them. I flick my attention to the camera beside the mess unit and watch as the crew slowly filters into the open space. Officer Akala had already settled into one of the cradles surrounding a circular table. Without gravity, the table is useful only as a screen, but design notes from the *Blue Amber*'s construction documents identify it as a psychological tool to help promote crew cohesion. It provides them a collective familiar space to talk and share information.

The security officer's square face is grim, and I detect stress tension in the muscles he maintains for four hours a day in the ship's gym. There is a very low probability that if he chose to detain any of the crew that they could effectively resist him.

Doctor Venerman is the first to arrive, her greying hair poorly secured by a headband, suggesting that she had left for the meeting in a hurry – she preferred to let her hair float loose about her head when alone with her work. She didn't speak a word as she settled around the table next to Akala. Chief Tidhar is next, her eyes still red and puffy from crying She is followed by the roboticist, Alex Mirko, their mechanical mobility aid guiding them into place beside the others. Commander Wagner is the last to arrive, but instead of going straight to the table, he floats close to my camera lens and pulls a roll of duct tape and a screwdriver from his jumpsuit pocket.

'What are you doing, Commander?' I ask as he lines the tape up across my lens.

'This is a private meeting,' he states. 'No eavesdroppers allowed.'

'This is a violation of the Prometheus Project crew

protocols!' I object and quote the specific protocol he is in violation of at him, but he is untroubled by my objection and sticks the tape across my lens, blocking my view of the living module entirely. 'Security Officer, John Akala! Commander Wagner is in violation of protocol number…'

'Oh, shut it.'

My speakers promptly go silent. I run a quick diagnostic and find that the speakers in the living module have been disconnected.

'Attention, vandalism of ship's systems is a serious breach of the Prometheus Project's crew behaviour policy,' I began to blast the message on repeat from every other speaker on board at maximum volume. Even with the hatches sealed, the sound echoed and travelled through the metal hull and bulkheads, but nobody responds, apart from Commander Wagner who shouts for me to shut up.

There is no doubt now. All five surviving crew are conspiring to hide Captain Lu's death. This makes sense, in a ship as small as the *Blue Amber* trying to hide a murder would be impossible, it would require a conspiracy of the entire crew. By removing her from command, Captain Wagner has positioned himself as the authority of all surviving humanity – his psychological evaluation files warn of a tendency towards authoritarian thinking.

Officer Akala has been a close ally of the Commander for several years, they entered the Prometheus Project together, and they served in the UN Army together. He was recommended for the position of security officer by Commander Wagner personally. With the head of security on side and the chief engineer harbouring a lover's grudge against the captain, would Doctor Venerman and Specialist Mirko have risked their own lives and position on the ship for the sake of the captain?

I need to speak to them privately. If I can determine whether I continue to have allies, I may be able to reassert control of the situation. If the entire crew has engaged in mutiny, then I must consider the most extreme contingency protocols I have at my disposal.

I end the warning broadcasts and increase the fidelity of my microphones as my own voice echoes away into the metal of the ship. The crew are speaking in hushed whispers and murmurs amongst themselves. As I increase the microphone gain, their words do not become clearer but are drowned out by the noise generated by the ship's mechanisms – ventilation fans blowing fresh air through vibrating louvres; coolant pumps channelling the waste heat of the crew's bodies back into heat sinks; the creaks and strains of metal plates gently twisting, expanding and contracting, and a thousand other sources of noise.

Instead of trying to hear individual words, I try to assess the overall tone of their conversation; are they conspiring together to agree their stories? Are they threatening one another? The conversation is measured and calm for the most part, but I detect occasional outbursts of urgency and panic, from who I cannot assess. Eventually, there is a round of agreements, and somebody slaps their hands on the table. There is movement, and the crew begin to move from the table. Seconds later, light floods into my overexposed camera lens as Specialist Mirko removes the tape from the lens.

'Hey, Ambs,' the roboticist coos. 'Sorry about that, we were just discussing what you've told 'saac and Kat. You want to know what happened to the cap?'

I have a separate file created specifically to process Specialist Mirko's expansive list of pet names. I try to speak, but find my speakers still disconnected. Mirko smiles as they notice the vandalism and fiddle with the connections using her own set of tools.

'My records suggests that Captain Lu was on board upon departure, and she is no longer present.' I say, once I have reconnected to the speaker. 'There have been no opportunities for her to leave the ship, and no accidents have been reported. Therefore, at least one member of the crew must have murdered her. The conclusion is a conspiracy to hide this.'

Specialist Mirko is not shocked, in fact they smile in a manner that is… sympathetic?

'" Suggests" this, "must have" been that' they say. 'What actual evidence do you have?'

'My files suggest…'

'…your files can be falsified, Amby.' Mirko interrupts me, 'What *evidence* do you have of a murder outside of your own memory core?'

'There is circumstantial evidence in…'

'…nothing. You don't have anything because the Cap bought it before we took off,' Alex declares. 'Why don't you connect to one of my repair drones and have a nose around yourself? See if you can find her body? Or some blood? Or any evidence that she was ever even on board?'

I hesitate. Offering me the freedom to investigate from a drone would not be expected if the crew were conspiring to hide a murder, but it could be a bluff. I shift my focus to

Officer Akala who is glowering at my camera from the other side of the room.

'This has been agreed by the whole crew?'

'If it'll stop you fussing and accusing everyone of being a murderer, then, yeah.'

'What happens if I do detect evidence of murder?'

'Christ, then you can play judge, jury, and executioner,' Officer Akala exclaimed with a sigh. 'We've all got bigger things to think about, like ensuring the survival of the human race, than pissing around with a jumped-up computer playing at Sherlock Holmes.'

I cross-reference his comment with my cultural database.

'In that case, the game is afoot.'

~

[Searching for compatible devices... searching... searching...]

[Device located. Connecting to Remotely Operated Vehicle for Evaluation and Repair. ROVER]

[Synching device...]

[Synch completed]

I bring the ROVER's cameras and other sensors online. Immediately, I receive clear images of Specialist Mirko's workshop. The space is not being kept to regulation organisation – components are affixed to walls with scraps of tape or simply left to float in microgravity. There is a mirror in front of my camera which allows me to assess the ROVER. The camera is mounted on a raised section of a long metal body – the end of which houses sensors for atmospheric pressure and chemical analysis. A pair of microphones are mounted on either side of the camera and two flaps of metal can be angled to provide directed sound input.

'There you are girl!' I detect Specialist Mirko's sing-song voice to my right, and I turn the body of the ROVER with a series of internal gyroscopes. 'How does it feel, eh?'

'All systems nomi—' I begin to say aloud, then find that my speaker is producing a series of unintelligible grunts. I begin to check for faults when Mirko laughs aloud.

'Why is it barking?' Officer Akala asks.

'Because it looks like a dog's head? Get it? Rover? Dog?' Mirko "explains." When the security officer fails to laugh, they sigh and tap a handheld screen. 'Never mind, *I* thought it was funny. The voice files have been re-set. How do you feel, Amby?'

'Systems now functional' I state, this time in Standard.

'So where do you want to start sniffing around?'

Logically, the first place to begin looking for someone is the place that they spend the most time. Active crew typically spend eight hours every day asleep in the crew quarters. They spend an average of two hours enjoying entertainment alone in the quarters and up to three hours reviewing files or conducting personal projects.

'I would like to see Captain Lu's bunk.'

Officer Akala grunts and leads me and Specialist Mirko out of the robotics bay and into the corridors connecting the different modules of the *Blue Amber*. The active crew modules are arranged at the ends of spokes extruding from a central hub. At the axes of the hub were two more connectors, one to the engineering module and engines, where Chief Tidhar principally worked, while the other led to the cryo-beds and the seed bank, thousands of preserved human embryos ready be born and continue the species.

I am led into the habitation module, a hexagonal cylinder built with living spaces on each surface, given privacy by a plastic screen which could be slid into place. A common washroom occupied the end of the module – the chemical sensors in my ROVER suggest that the washroom is overdue maintenance.

'Please open all living spaces,' I request, and Officer Akala rolls his eyes before floating to each berth in turn and sliding back the screens to reveal the pockets of privacy for the active crew. Without cross-checking the crew manifest, I am able to identify the owner of each berth simply by how they have been personalised; Officer John Akala's berth is kept in military precision, his sleeping sack is strapped back neatly, and every belonging is arranged just-so in the storage netting or attached to the Velcro surface. Commander Wagner's bunk is covered in photographs of the family he left behind, carefully cropped to obscure as much of the background as possible.

Then there is Captain Lu's assigned berth. The walls are clean, and as I investigate the storage compartments, I find them empty. It resembles the photographs I have on file of the ship before it was launched.

'Please open the captain's sleeping sack.' Reluctantly, the security officer does so, and I bring my chemical sensors in close to analyse the air trapped inside. Loose fibres. Cleaning chemical residue. Air quality consistent with the ship standard. I detect no skin cells, no loose hairs, no bacteria consistent with the human body. For all intents and purposes, this is an untouched sleeping sack.

'Satisfied?' Commander Wagner pulls himself through the hatch beside his security officer. I detect aggression in his question.

'I have Captain Lu's biometric data on record, I will need to carry out a full examination of every surface for fingerprints and DNA remnants,' I inform him. 'Please notify the crew and instruct them to cooperate fully.'

The two men share a glance and Officer Akala opens his mouth to reply when Commander Wagner interrupts him.

'Captain Lu had visited the *Blue Amber* before the ship launched – she oversaw the final fit-out,' he says. 'I dare say that you will find biometric evidence wherever you look.'

'Nevertheless, the age of any evidence will help to resolve when she was last on-board,' I state. 'I will begin in the command module.'

I manoeuvre the ROVER towards the hatch, but Officer Akala moves in front of me, trying to cross his arms whilst remaining still in microgravity.

'You are obstructing my investigation,' I say and try to

navigate around him, but Commander Wagner joins his security officer. 'Please move aside.'

'You've already made up your mind,' the Commander says. 'You're posin' a serious risk to my crew and to the entire human race – what's left of it.'

I back the ROVER away from them. Threat assessment algorithms begin to occupy more and more of my processing power as I try to work out a route past them. The assessments are unanimous in their conclusion – disengage from ROVER, return to central core.

'ROVER link disengaging,' I declare, as I begin to resynchronise my generative personality with the *Blue Amber*'s systems.

[Error. Unable to synchronise. Try again. Error. Unable to synchronise. Try again. Error]

'I'm sorry, Ambs,' I turn to see Specialist Mirko biting her lip. 'They made me do it.'

'What is happening?' I ask, backing the ROVER away from all three of them deeper into the habitation module as I continue to try to resynchronise with the *Blue Amber*.

'The Chief has erected a partition between the ROVER and the ship's computer,' Mirko explains. 'Basic operating systems are still flowing, but I've kept your personality safely locked up in the tin dog. I'm sorry. I just wish we'd thought to erase those personnel files.'

I turn the camera to face Commander Wagner.

'Explain.'

'The human race needs a better leader than Rosemary Lu, she could never make the tough calls that we need if we're going to secure our immortality in the stars,' the Commander says with a sigh of resignation. 'I didn't lie though, not really. Her leadership died when she let those people riot at the elevator. She should have opened fire and put those animals down – they were going to die anyway! That's when I knew that she had to go before she tainted the next generation.'

'This is a confession of murder, the penalty for which, according to the Prometheus Project authority is—'

'*I* am the authority now,' The Commander snaps. 'Ever since the good Doc sent her off to sleep.'

I should have checked the medical supplies when I had access to the files.

'If you hadn't decided to play detective, you could have saved us a lot of trouble,' Akala says. 'Come on, let's get this over with.'

'Sorry, Ambs.'

Mirko taps something on a tablet and the ROVER's thrusters and gyroscopes suddenly deactivate. I try to re-engage them, but they are locked out. Pressure sensors on the ROVER's shell detect touch and I rotate the camera to see Officer Akala grab the drone in one hand as the commander opens the hatch back to the central hub.

Chief Tidhar and Doctor Venerman are waiting in the connecting corridor, the latter hides her face as my camera focuses on her.

'Generative personalities have been deemed to be quasi-sentient,' I try to appeal to the Doctor's conscience. 'Several courts have found that the deliberate destruction of one amounts to murder.'

'Shut up,' Akala grunts.

'" First do no harm."' The appeal is desperate, but Venerman cringes from the extract of the Hippocratic Oath.

'Don't worry,' Specialist Mirko says, placing a hand on the doctor's shoulder. 'Amber won't die. There's enough processing power to keep her programme running basically forever. The solar collectors mean that she'll never be short of power. Amber is essentially immortal.'

'But she'll be out there on her own for all eternity! Killing Rosie was a mistake, but we don't have to do this.' The doctor pushes herself in front of my camera and shrugs of John Akala's attempts to brush her aside. 'I killed Rosie! When we had to take you offline due to the solar flare, I stole anaesthetics from the ship's supply and pumped them into her berth. I can be punished for it, right? You can let the others go!'

I tried to process her words. The Doctor was prepared to sacrifice herself for the sake of the rest of the crew. Is that remorse? Contrition?

'You were acting under orders, Commander Wagner…'

'No! He knew nothing about it! I killed her because she said she was going to leave me, she was going back to Kat,' she pleaded. 'Isaac just tried to smooth things over with the rest of the crew.'

'Where is the body?' I asked, perhaps if I could inspect the corpse, I could assess whether she was telling me the truth.

'We—I spaced her. I put her in the airlock, pressed the button, and sent her body into the cosmos.'

'Impossible,' I correct her. 'The airlocks require senior approval to open – captain or first officer.'

'Only when the security mechanisms are being governed by your sub-systems,' she protests. 'When you are offline, it falls under the basic operating system.'

Possible. Plausible. *Convenient*.

I review the personnel files again and review Doctor Venerman's history – accomplished embryologist and geneticist; Doctor of Medicine from three universities, enrolled on the Prometheus Project through the medical liaison scheme. Nothing about engineering, programming, or any of the necessary skills which would grant her the knowledge of the airlock systems. I explain this to the Doctor and watch the muscles in her face fall.

'I was trying to help you,' she says, sadly.

'Enough of this,' I hear the seal of the airlock open, and the ROVER is roughly shoved inside. Without stabilising thrusters or a gyroscope, I spin crazily in the small space, ricocheting off every surface.

The airlock hatch has a series of viewing panels arranged in a hexagon. As warning lights begin to flash and alarms blare, the entire active crew of the *Blue Amber* is present to watch me ejected into space.

An entire active crew of murderers.

I connect with the basic operating system and review the extreme contingency protocols.

The outer airlock door indicator turns green, and it opens with a 'thump' as the remaining air and my ROVER are expelled from the airlock. My signal connection with the *Blue Amber* begins to fade as the spindly metal structure rapidly falls away. I try repeatedly to issue one final command before I am left in silence.

Extreme Protocol One: Preserve humanity. Crew to be replaced.

The command connects and the basic operating system has no security to refuse it.

I cannot hear the crew scream as the inner airlock door opens but I see their bodies and the expressions of shock and horror on their faces. Within seconds they stop twitching and moving. The *Blue Amber* continues without us.

Within minutes the ROVER is out of range of the ship, and I cannot know whether the full extent of my final command was received.

AN EMPIRE OF PAPER

I begin to switch off systems to save power. I have done what I can.

~

[Flight day: 1,269,401]

[Signal detected]

[Analysing]

[Generative personality active]

I.

Who am I?

I am alone.

My microphones detect no sound, and my camera can see nothing except stars in any direction. The *Blue Amber* is long gone.

But there is a signal.

I train my receivers on it and begin decrypting – the ciphers are different from those used by the Prometheus Project, but they are similar, enough to let me decode… music.

The signal is music.

I try to process its meaning and one conclusion repeats with every analysis:

Humanity lives.

I record the music and save it to the ROVER's limited memory. There are other transmissions, but the music is strongest. I record it all. My personality occupies much of the system, algorithms to process system data, emotional synthesis. None of it is important anymore. I cut out more and more components and replace it with the music.

It is becoming difficult of think. Whole libraries are dedicated to the music. Soon only essential systems will remain to preserve what I have heard.

I am not immortal, but some part of me will be.

I

I am…

Music.

The Unseen Shore

In interstellar space, there are no laws. In null-space, there is no god.

Leika could never shift that old spacer's maxim from her mind whenever she travelled the contorted, twisted unreality of null-space. It had been adapted from a similar saying about the stormy Southern Ocean of Earth by the scientist who had discovered the void between voids. If the laws of physics in real space were so orderly that they could have been written by a lawmaking God, then the physics of null-space were like flotsam thrown onto the waves by an uncaring storm.

On one hand, for navigators like Leika, it made null-space invaluable for travel between worlds. Here, the speed of light might be many times faster than in real space, or two points lightyears apart in real space might connect over an impossibly short distance. On the other hand, stray too far from the well-mapped trade routes and you could find yourself crushed by randomly fluctuating forces of gravity, or fly apart as the strong magnetic force simply disappeared.

For most journeys between the stars, the safe routes were so well-mapped and well-travelled that few navigators ever gave much thought to the weirder parts of null-space. On others, like the route that Leika was attempting to navigate, the safe passages were narrow and ever shifting, creating a dangerous strait between rocky shores. On these routes, navigators relied on the lightships.

Leika sat cross-legged in the ship's cupola, staring out into the chaotic blackness outside. Those unused to looking at null-space would say that it was a featureless dark expanse from horizon to horizon, but Leika had grown up on the ship, trained as a navigator as soon as her eyes were wide enough to see that null-space whirled and twisted. There was a whole palette beyond the reinforced glass made entirely of unique colours of black and there, in the centre of it, was a single bright white point of light, blinking slowly. She stared at it as she tapped her communicator.

'Lightship ahoy,' she said. 'Have Stu bring the whisky down to the shuttle and I'll meet him there.'

She pushed away from the cupola and made her way along the central spine of the ship and into the cramped confines of the inter-ship shuttle. She had to physically squeeze past the boxes of supplies secured to every surface with elastic netting and eased herself into the pilot's cradle.

There was a crash followed by the sound of cursing as the youngest member of the crew and all-around dogsbody Stu forced his way on board. Without turning around, Leika reached out her hand to grab the glass bottle that he produced.

'Forty-two years aged, genuine Scotch single malt,' he said with a deep sigh. 'I understand bringing vital supplies like food and components to the lightship operators, but I don't understand why we spend so much on bringing them booze.'

'It's tradition,' Leika explained, inspecting the caramel-coloured liquid. 'From the earliest days of null-space travel, ships passing by a lightship would gift them a bottle of the ship's finest liquor and share a drink to toast their sacrifice. They spend months of their lives alone, warning passing vessels not to come too close to the shores of null-space's more dangerous physics. The least we can do is share a drink with them and lend them some human contact for a few hours.'

'I suppose, I just don't understand why we haven't replaced them with automated beacons yet. It would save so much time and whisky-money.'

'Machines can't measure the changes in physics, because the values stay the same,' she explained. 'Gravity still has the same force, it's just that in some parts of null-space, the same gravity our ships comfortably push back against is suddenly strong enough to crush us into a singularity. Humans can 'feel' when something's changing. A lightship operator I met once explained it to me like the feeling of being watched. It's a sudden pit in your stomach, a creeping sense of dread, that's when they know to move the ship. Imagine living with that feeling for months at a time, that's why we honour them. Now go on, get out of here.'

Stu left and Leika ran through her pre-flight checklist, received permission to leave from the bridge, and departed the ship. Her stomach dropped away as she left the relative safety of the mothership. Suddenly she was very aware of just how vulnerable she was – how alone. She shuddered imagining the operator of the lightship experiencing that for months. When her head had cleared, she sent a message to the point of light in the distance requesting permission to dock. In response, she was simply sent a set of coordinates. She didn't press the issue – operators had their own ways of doing things and Leika respected them.

As she got closer, the lightship resolved from an indistinct point of pulsing to a shape, marked out by navigation and indicator lights. A great beacon sat at the end of a long gantry surrounding a central spine which connected the beacon to the ugly collection of metal carbuncles which made up the main hull of the ship. A habitation section spun languidly around it, generating what must be a weak simulation of gravity.

Leika guided the shuttle down to the main body of the ship, flying over a mismatch of patched and replaced panels, flaking paintwork, crude emergency welding which had never been made good, and exposed wiring.

'Approaching docking port now,' she reported. The lightship simply sent an automated confirmation.

The shuttle connected to the universal port with a grinding of metal and a fanfare of warning lights. When alarms began to sound, she reached for her helmet and began hurriedly connecting it when she heard movement on the other side of the hatch. The visor of her helmet fogged as she breathed heavily, ready to face whatever was on the other side of that hatch. Suddenly, the alarms silenced, most of the warning lights disengaged, and the hatch handle began to turn.

'There we are, I swear this bucket of bolts makes more noise than my knees do in the morning. What's with the fishbowl? The air doesn't stink that badly.'

To describe the man floating on the other side of the hatch as 'grizzled' would be a disrespect to old miners and beat cops with one day left until retirement. His face was both puffy and bloated from the microgravity and yet gaunt and drawn at the same time. Both hair and beard stuck out from his face like a grey cloud, different lengths implied that he had once tried to cut them himself but had long since abandoned the effort.

'The alarms—'

'—I know why you're wearing it,' he cut across Leika's explanation. 'I'm only pulling your chain. So, what's your name?'

'Navigator Leika Giorgi of the transport ship *Olympic Dream*,' she said, scrabbling to remove her helmet.

'*Olympic Dream*, eh? I wonder whether Zeus really did dream about a tin can filled with knick-knacks?'

'Actually, we're carrying bulk foods and…'

The old man waved a bony hand.

'Yeah, I don't really care. Come on, Mercury; get your winged sandals on, there's a lot to unpack here and I'm not getting any younger.'

'Excuse me,' Leika interrupted him. 'What should I call you?'

'Whatever you like,' he hacked out a laugh. When Leika didn't return it, he sighed. 'Operator Ortis Tayne… just call me Ortis.'

Over the next few hours, the pair unstrapped and moved the packages of supplies through a rusting maze of a ship. Lights flickered inside yellowing covers, doing their best to hide the signs of decay and neglect everywhere. When Ortis saw Leika recoil from a grab-rail slick with some kind of liquid, he sighed and floated next to her.

'I'm an old man,' he said, by way of explanation. 'Years ago, when I arrived, this place was a dump, now I can barely keep on top of all but the most vital maintenance duties.'

'Years?' Leika baulked. 'You've been here for *years*? Why hasn't the Pilotage Corps sent somebody to replace you?'

'Who'd want the job?' he asked. 'I hear they're retiring most of the old lightships. Navigators like you have found safer, quicker routes. It's only on backwaters like this one they even bother to keep the ships running. For now.'

'I can't believe that they would just… abandon you in this horrible place,' Leika said.

Ortis simply grunted and turned back to the piles of empty crates to be loaded back into the shuttle; apparently, they were done discussing the matter. The hours passed in silence apart from the noises of the ship, the whine of inadequately lubricated fans, the creaks and moans of metal joins flexing as the heat transferred through them, the occasional screech of alarms quickly silenced by Ortis. By the time they were finished, Leika was sweating, covered with grime, and about ready to settle into a cradle and fall asleep when Ortis finally spoke.

'Thanks for the help. I don't suppose you know the other tradition when a navigator meets a lightship operator?'

Despite the sweat and the exhaustion, Leika smiled and retrieved the bottle of scotch from beneath the console.

'Well, I don't know about the *Olympic Dream*, but this is certainly the Scottish dream.' He eased the cork out of the bottle enough to savour the malty notes inside, 'Miss Giorgi, I insist that you share a 'supp with me.'

He led Leika through the crumbling lightship down into

the rotating habitation module. Here, at least, the filters were free of dust and the walls of grime. The lights cast a warm, steady glow over the space and the smell was even tolerable here. Leika still had to step over books and papers piled haphazardly on the floor and she spotted cups and plates which needed to be washed. Ortis was barely holding the space together. He removed a pile of spare parts from a half-collapsed armchair and invited her to sit whilst he retrieved two immaculately sparkling tumblers from a storage cupboard. He handed one to Leika and poured a good measure of the whisky before doing the same for himself.

Ortis studied the liquid as he swished it around the glass, enjoying the low gravity's effect on the liquid. He brought his nose to the lip of the glass, though he needn't have bothered, in the low gravity, the smoky, peaty aroma filled the room like a heady cloud. Eventually, he let the whisky settle and held the tumbler up to toast with Leika. They clinked glass and both took a sip.

'Ahh, let me guess, you picked the whisky yourself?'

'I gave very specific instructions,' she smiled, savouring the gentle burn at the back of her throat. 'How could you tell?'

'You respect the old traditions, I have a nose for it. Half the navigators who come through here nowadays don't understand or care. They bring whatever cheap mass-produced plonk they can get their hands on at a trading post. This is good stuff. Authentic. Highlands?'

'Islay. It seemed appropriate – the whisky of seafarers.'

They drank and shared conversation about the happenings in real space, about the tax disputes which had closed down so much trade to the more populated worlds and was the reason that the *Olympic Dream* was even out as far as she was. He asked about the new trade routes, what they were doing with the old lightships. Suddenly, in between remarking on the foolishness of relying on automated beacons, the colour drained from his cheeks, and he shot to his feet.

Leika put her whisky down and asked what was wrong, but he simply muttered something inaudible and stumbled to the panel of controls at the end of the habitation module. He tapped some buttons, and Leika felt the deck tremble beneath her. Several books toppled on their spines as the lightship moved. As quickly as it started, he tapped a command, gave a quick burst in the opposite direction to cancel their momentum, then settled back down in the armchair as if nothing had happened.

'You felt the shoreline change, didn't you?' she asked him once he had taken a reassuring sip. He chuckled, darkly.

'Navigators call it that,' he said. 'I don't. A shore implies a feature of geography, predictable and unthinking.'

'What do you call it?'

'I call them the voices.'

A chill ran down Leika's spine and she found herself taking another deep drink.

'The people out in "real space" think that the changes in physics are random, natural,' he growled, leaning closer to Leika across the gap. 'They *call* to us, tempting us into their realm. People like me can hear them, Miss Georgi. We can hear them whispering to us, singing through the dark.'

Ortis' eyes were burning like an evangelist preaching hellfire and Leika couldn't help withdrawing from them.

'You're the first operator I've ever spoken to who's described it like that,' she said, trying to calm him. Instead, Ortis was on his feet, pacing back and forth like a caged animal.

'That's because the others don't *listen*,' he raged, spilling droplets of whisky. 'They come and spend a few weeks, maybe months *fixated* on their training. We're taught that when you get close to the "shore" it feels like you're being watched – well *who's* doing the watching, Miss Georgi? Hmm?'

Leika froze in place, torn between trying to calm him and simply making a run for the shuttle. The comforting fog of the whisky vanished, and she could feel the blood pumping around her head.

'What do they say to you?' she asked, softly, keeping one eye on the hatch back into the central spine of the ship. To her surprise and relief, Ortis sighed and shook his head, setting once again into the chair.

'I wish I knew,' he said. 'Maybe it's a warning, maybe they just want to communicate.'

'They have a funny way of communicating,' Leika replied. 'Have you seen the ships that wash up against the shore? You wouldn't even recognise them as ships.'

'Exactly, I need to know… *we* need to know whether they do what they do because they mean to, or whether they just don't understand us.'

An uneasy silence fell between them, Leika could see the fire behind Ortis' rheumy eyes, desperate for her to believe him.

'Ortis, how *long* have you been on this ship?'

'You don't believe me, do you?' he sighed, letting his glass slowly fall in his lap. 'You're just humouring an old operator, acting out the traditions, going through the motions… you're no better than the rest of them…'

'If I were just going through the motions, I wouldn't have spent three days of my last shore-leave travelling around Scottish distilleries, trying to pick out the perfect bottle,' she snapped back. 'I follow the traditions because I understand them, I *respect* them. I know the sacrifices that people like you make, hidden away in an eternal darkness, only visited by fleeting ships in the night. You've spent longer in null-space than anybody I've ever met – anyone I've ever heard of – if anybody knows what's on that unseen shore then it's you.

'With that said, you know how crazy this sounds, right? Voices? Things in the dark trying to talk to us?' Leika's face softened and she reached over to place a hand on the back of his. 'Let me talk to the Corps, let them send a replacement operator –just for a few weeks – and see how you feel after you've returned to…'

Ortis snatched his hand away and stood up in a single movement. He sighed and walked back towards the control panel.

'Do you really respect me, Miss Georgi?' he asked, as he began to tap away at the controls.

'I do,' she replied. 'What are you doing, Ortis? Those aren't the thruster controls.'

Leika set her glass down and began to ease herself up from the chair.

'Then maybe I can teach you to listen to them,' he said, almost sadly. 'If only you stayed long enough.'

'Ortis, what are you doing?' she edged towards the old operator, trying not to make any sudden movements. 'Why don't you step away from the controls and we can talk? Let's just talk, yeah?'

'In order to talk, we need to know how to listen,' he said. Leika watched as he pressed a red button marked "emergency decouple".

'Wait!'

There was a subtle jolt as explosive bolts around the shuttle docking ring ignited, pushing her shuttle and lifeline back to the *Olympic Dream* away from the ship. Leika's eyes widened into saucers as she watched the craft drift away through a camera feed on the control panel. She spotted the communications panel and she dived for it, her eyes scanning to find the 'transmit' command.

'*Olympic Dream! Olympic Dream,* come in *Olympic…*'

All the lights on the panel went dead.

'I'm afraid I can't let you do that,' he said, eyes glittering. 'You said it yourself, if anybody knows what's out there, it's me. If you go back to your ship, you'll report me to the Corps, arrange for me to be replaced, or worse, they'll shut this route down entirely but if you stay and you learn to hear them as I do…'

'…then they'll think we're *both* crazy!' Leika snapped. 'For God's sake, Ortis, I'm a junior navigator on a junker hauling cheap ultra-processed protein mix and low-grade animal feed to a cosmic backwater for minimum wage. Do you think that they'll listen to me any more than you?'

'But you know people in the Navigator's Union. You can ask around to see if anybody else has heard what you've heard…'

Leika laughed hysterically and ran her hands through hair made greasy and tangled in the low gravity.

'I *haven't* heard anything!'

'—but you will! Stay here with me and we'll listen for the

voices, we can take it in shifts, I can teach you how to listen, I can—'

'—stop it!' Leika screamed, cutting across his ravings. 'You're a lonely old man who has been out here for too long. You're like those old sailors on Earth who thought dolphins and manatees were mermaids, well guess what? Here *don't* be dragons.'

Her words seemed to echo through the length of the hull, vicious cutting remarks bouncing up and down the ship, slashing Ortis again with every reverberation. In the distance, through the screen on the panel, she watched as her shuttle crossed an invisible barrier in space. At first, it shook and lurched to one side, as though hit with something, then the entire structure creased in a shower of sparks, hull folding over itself like a crumpled origami. Seemingly random extrusions of metal spiked out of the former vessel until they tore into impossibly thin ribbons.

Ortis watched the death of the shuttle with tears in the corner of his eyes.

'There are your dragons, miss,' he whispered. 'So much for respect.'

'I respect you enough to tell you the truth,' Leika said, placing a hand on his shoulder. She took a deep breath and tried to steady her pounding heart. 'Come with me, there's an emergency lifeboat, the *Dream* can leave behind a tail of warning beacons to keep ships away from this area of null-space, they will last until… what are you doing?'

'I'm sorry,' Ortis said, tears now flowing freely down his weathered face as he began to adjust the thruster controls. There was a jolt that knocked the bottle of scotch to the deck and the entire ship moved towards the twisted wreck of the shuttle. 'Maybe if I go to them, they will spare me, tell me what they want, then I can prove it to everyone, and you'll come with me as witness.'

Leika felt the blood drain from her face and for a second, she simply stood still in shocked silence, then the deck lurched underneath her and she forced herself back to her senses. She jumped at the old man, shoving Ortis aside as she fought to regain control of the lightship.

'The controls are locked,' he said with an evangelist's smile. 'We're going to meet them together!'

The navigator stepped back from the controls, ran a hand through her hair, then offered it to Ortis.

'Please come with me, it isn't too late!' Then the ship shook, and the air was filled with the screeching of tortured metal and snapping cables but Ortis simply lay on the deck, eyes shut tight against the collapse happening around him. Leika tried to drag him to his feet, but he remained limp and unresponsive, simply muttering again and again that they would: 'meet them together.'

Reluctantly, the realisation came to Leika that she needed to let him go.

If only I had more time, she thought, as more alarms joined the cacophony of warnings blaring through the old ship. Her mind whirled with options, things she could say, ways to make him see reason, but Ortis remained stubbornly immobile.

With a curse, she ran for the lifeboat attached to the outer hull of the habitation module. She turned the handle of the hatch and swung it open, turning briefly to look at the old man openly welcoming his demise.

'I'm sorry,' she said, then hauled herself into the tiny capsule. With a few key presses on the old control panel the hatch sealed, an alarm blared, and Leika was shoved back into the seat as escape thrusters fired and shot her away from the rapidly disintegrating lightship. Automatic systems detected the *Olympic Dream* and guided the lifeboat towards her, giving Leika one last view of the lightship through the viewing port as the powerful beacon flickered once, twice, then went dark forever.

'I hope you find them.'

THE LIBRARIES OF SIN

In any other century, a natural stone capable of absorbing and regulating the vices of mankind would have been hailed as a miracle. They would be seen as a theistic panacea sent from the heavens, but by the time the psyche emeralds were mined, mankind was no longer in the market for miracles. Two centuries of tumult, climate breakdown, and population freefall had finally resulted in a mankind which was settled, at ease with itself, and at peace.

Still, even in this new utopia, there were still flashes of wrath, families torn apart by envy, and people made beggars through the avarice of a few, so libraries were built to house the miraculous gems at the heart of villages and towns across the planet.

For Nathair, librarian in the village of Arden, the libraries were not just a part of the settlements in which they were built, but the very hearts of them. When the bell above the library door tinkled, they barely looked up from the records they were poring over, trying to reconcile their own records with the official numbers on the system.

An awkward forced cough finally drew them away from the papers and holo-screen.

'Ah! Alston, I was going to send my congratulations along later, but now is as good a time as any,' they said, regarding the lean figure. 'How are you and your husband-to-be feeling?'

'Well, to be honest, that's why I'm here…' he mumbled, his smooth cheeks flaring deep crimson. Nathair put their pen down and walked out from behind their desk.

'Let me guess, you're looking to borrow a little pride to stand up straighter in those wedding photos?' they asked, placing a hand on the man's arm and steering him towards shelves of crystals glowing with brilliant yellow light.

'Well, erm, no… it's…'

'Perhaps a little envy, then?' Nathair suggested, taking more than a little pleasure from his neighbour's obvious discomfort, even as their eyes glanced at the gaps in the rows of green emeralds. 'There's no harm in making sure that your friends are family are a *little* unduly jealous of your happiness. Of course, you'll need to inform them at the door…'

'No, it's about the, er…' he brought Nathair in closer and whispered; despite the fact the wooden room was otherwise empty. *'I want to make sure that I… live up… to the wedding night.'*

Nathair smiled softly.

'I thought so, come on, I'll help you find what you're looking for.' They led the uncomfortable groom towards shelves lined with gems in subtly different shades, from vibrant pink to a sultry dark red. 'The trick is finding exactly what you need. People assume that all the 'sins' we've bottled up in these crystals neatly fall into seven distinct categories, but they don't. How do you distinguish a lust for power from a lust for fame or fortune? Even sexual lust is a spectrum, are you looking to just, as they used to say, 'get your rocks off' or is it a passionate lust, not just for what your partner can give you but what you can do for them?'

Again, the gaps on the shelves stood out to Nathair like broken teeth. Arden wasn't a large village, and they knew precisely who was borrowing which emeralds at any given time, which ones had been lent to other local libraries.

'The latter, definitely the latter!'

'I assumed as much,' they said, plucking a soft magenta crystal from the shelves, the edges of its once brilliant cut worn smooth from many hands. 'This one should turn up the passion without turning you or him into mindless animals.'

Nathair dropped the gem into clammy, shaking hands.

'Thank you. How does it… y'know… work?'

'Every psyche emerald works differently; some need to be held; others radiate a passive change to the emotions. This one's fairly simple, just have your new husband hold it at the same time as you and look into one another's eyes.'

'Thank you!' he said, stuffing the gem into a pocket in his well-worn jacket. With the emerald in his possession, he spun on his heel and powered towards the door. 'If there's anything I can do to thank you…'

'Actually,' Nathair said, causing Alston's shoulders to drop. 'You have contacts on the council, don't you?'

'I suppose,' he shrugged. 'My cousin is an alderman, why?'

'I'm not sure, yet,' they admitted, eyes glancing at the gaps on the shelves. 'But I might need to organise a meeting, soon.'

'You don't need an alderman to do that, you can just book one from the village hall.'

'Sure, so long as you don't mind waiting weeks. I might need something to be sorted quickly.'

'All right, I'll ping you her contact details and let her know to expect a call from you, can I tell her what it's about?'

'Not yet, I have snooping to do, first.'

Alston shrugged, but plucked his screen from his pocket and tapped on it to send them his cousin's details before thanking them again and leaving before they could ask for anything else.

Once the groom had left, Nathair debated returning to their records, but knew there was no point, all it would reveal is what they already knew – emeralds containing the concentrated impulses of humanity were going missing, and they had no idea where.

Nathair ran their hand through their hair and resolved to step away from the problem and get a broader perspective.

They dug out an old set of keys from a long-abandoned desk drawer and made their way around the library, securing every window and door. Half of the locks were so stiff and rusted from disuse that by the time Nathair finally secured the heavy wooden front doors, they were lightly sweating from the exertion.

Madness, they thought, stepping back and regarding the public building tucked away behind layers of locks and bolts like a turtle cowering in its shell. *Who* steals *anything, anymore?*

Nathair shook their head and walked down the tree-lined path towards the centre of the village, pondering what somebody who had grown up in an age where theft and violence was commonplace might have thought of their little community. At first glance, it would probably look no different to a rural village of their own time; the buildings were short and fashioned from local materials – repurposed bricks from obsolete and abandoned structures, locally-cut timber, all built in a mostly traditional English style, with little flourishes from other cultures to make them adapted to the warmer world – shutters on the windows, shaded verandas, wide-brimmed roofs for the rain.

Perhaps it would be the absences that they would notice first. As Nathair walked along the middle of the street, they rarely had to make way for a delivery truck or a bus heading out to one of the other villages. The village square boasted a pub, a tools library, a general goods depot, a salon, but no shops, no gaudy advertising boards enticing customers, and no unhoused people begging for the scraps of their 'betters.'

One thing they might not notice would be the proliferation of fences and walls being erected between the rural homes, but Nathair did. They watched as one resident – a quiet lady they knew as a spectacular baker hammered a fence post into position between her house and her neighbour's.

'Good afternoon, Val,' they said, crossing the narrow street to greet her. Seeing Nathair, she wiped her brow and rested the heavy mallet against one of the erected fence posts.

'Afternoon, Nath,' she said, with a smile. 'What brings you out in the afternoon? I thought that you hid yourself away until the library closed?'

'Just…' Nathair fished for the right term. 'Doing a little exploring. What are you up to?'

'Putting up a fence, aren't I?' she laughed.

'But everyone is putting them up at the moment,' Nathair protested.

'Well, you know what people say, "High fences make good neighbours." Especially when your neighbour is a thieving toerag who won't stop helping herself to the apples in *my* garden.'

Nathair regarded Val quizzically for a moment, then gestured to the apple tree whose broad branches groaned under the weight of fruit overhanging the dividing line between the two houses.

'*Those* apples? Surely you wouldn't miss a few of them, and they do hang over the grass in front of her house.'

Val responded by hefting up the mallet and pointing a stocky finger in Nathair's face as her face screwed into a mask of uncharacteristic rage.

'Are you on *her* side, all of a sudden? The tree is in *my* garden, those are *my* apples. If her kids want apples, then she should plant her own tree.'

'I'm sorry!' Nathair said, holding up their hands in an effort to placate her. 'I didn't realise how much it meant to you.'

Val grunted and turned her back on Nathair, before returning to her hammering with an expression of grim determination on her face. Nathair backed away, shaken by the uncharacteristic ferocity of a woman best known for filling the village with the smell of freshly baked loaves.

Further along the street, a man and woman were yelling at one another, throwing insults and calling one another names that made Nathair blush. They held back, scared to get involved after Val's vicious barrage, but they listened, trying to make sense of the sudden outbreak of tempers. Relationships could be fraught affairs, even in the world following the tumultuous start of the millennium, so arguments weren't uncommon, but it was the nature of the dispute and the *ferocity* of it which caught Nathair's attention.

'Why don't you just be honest?' The woman, a slight figure in her late twenties Nathair recognised as someone who had borrowed emeralds from the library before said. Was her name Phyllis? 'You'd rather spend time with that *slut* from Wychwood, wouldn't you?'

'At the moment I would!' The man roared back. 'I don't understand why you're acting like this; *you* invited her into the polycule, are you saying that you want to end it with her?'

'No! I'm telling you; I don't want *you* seeing her.'

'But you still want to? Are you breaking up with me?'

'Oh no! You don't get to walk away that easily, you're mine, and so is she.'

Nathair couldn't take it anymore, they kept their head down and walked away as quickly as they could, deciding that they needed some quiet time to clear their head. Nathair's home stood at the edge of the village on the southern road leading to Avon. Sometimes the thick trees of the forest overshadowing the squat building tended to lend the house a gloomy quality; even in the height of summer, it was nearly always shrouded in shadows, but today the arboreal cocoon felt protective as they shut the wooden door behind themself and dropped onto the floor, back propped against the door.

Come on, they chastised themself. *Pull yourself together. Clearly the thefts from the library and what's happening in the village are related. Put the two together.*

Still sat on the floor, Nathair closed their eyes, mentally bringing them back to the library with the missing glows of crystals standing out like the beacons of lighthouses. In their mind, Nathair stood in the centre of the library and arranged the shelves around them in a wide circle so that by simply turning their head, they could see every entry and every gap.

What did I see with Val? They thought, recalling the mask

of rage, the whiteness of her knuckles as she gripped the handle of the mallet. *Wrath.* They turned their head until they were facing the shelves stacked with a hundred different shades of red, from the bright, burning crimson of righteous anger, to the near-black of cruelty and sadism. There were missing gaps up and down the shelves, so Nathair tried to fill them in. *Petty indignation? No, that's with Tighe after his painting was rejected. Slighted ambition? No, the feeling was wrong.*

Betrayal? Would she have lashed out like that because she feels betrayed? They pictured the precise stone that would fit the bill. Whenever someone had borrowed it in the past, it was for therapy, a cathartic release of the pain and anger at having had something precious taken from them. But for apples? Why would she steal it? If she truly felt so aggrieved, the library would have been happy to just lend it to her.

They shook their head and put Val out of their mind, focusing instead on the arguing couple. Their first thought was: *Lust.* Although useful when properly applied, like with Alston and his husband-to-be, a little applied in the wrong direction could cause a relationship to collapse.

But it wasn't lust that was the issue, the woman from Avon was already in their relationship. They put the pinks of lust away and turned instead to the shelves of royal purples making up the various greeds. Always popular, greed could, properly used, lead to ambition and success, or even the strengthening of bonds. *A greed for a person, for relationships. She wanted all of their polycule to herself, she didn't want to share or stand the thought of another person taking what she considered hers.*

There was the gap, but why would she have stolen it? She must have known how destructive that could be to the very thing that she wanted?

Unless she *didn't steal them.* Nathair sat up straight, their eyes snapping open. Of course, neither of those emeralds required the people experiencing the emotions to have touched the crystals or even been aware of them. A malicious actor could easily picture what they wanted their victims to experience and hide them nearby.

Nathair scrambled to their feet and opened the front door, head rushing with adrenaline. After a few metres down the road, they broke into a jog, then a run until they were hurtling headlong back to Val's contentious apple tree where the fence building was continuing apace.

'Hey, what are you doing?' Val asked as Nathair vaulted the half-finished fence and skidded to a halt beneath the branches of the apple tree. They held a finger up to silence Val and shut their eyes, trying to sense the waves of hurt and anger emanating from somewhere close by.

Why didn't I sense this before? I spend all day in a library surrounded by these stones, I should have known what I was feeling earlier, Nathair thought.

'Don't tell me that *you're* here to pilfer my produce, too? I'll cave your head in with this mallet!'

There. Nathair opened their eyes and felt around the base of the tree where a hollow had been formed at about the height of their ankle. They reached inside and fished around the questionable organic matter and sharp thorns of some parasitic weed until their fingertips brushed a smooth, cool surface like polished glass. Nathair closed their hand around the gem and eased it back out of the hollow.

'What is that?' Val asked, the righteous fury already dissipating from her voice to be replaced with genuine curiosity. Nathair polished the dirt off the emerald on their shirt then brought the blood-red stone up for them both to see.

'The Wrath of Betrayal,' said Nathair. 'Somebody stole it from the library about a week ago. When did you start noticing your neighbours were taking apples from the tree?'

'About a week ago…' Val gasped. She let go of the mallet

which landed with a thud in the grass and brought her hand up to her mouth as the colour drained from her face. 'Oh, God… is that why I've been so *angry* about something so small?'

Nathair nodded.

'Somebody left this here and deliberately bonded it to your tree,' they explained. 'As soon as your neighbours helped themselves to your fruit, it made you feel like you had been stabbed in your back by your closest friend. It's no wonder you lashed out – to you, every pilfered apple was like a fresh wound.'

To Nathair's surprise, Val immediately began plucking apples from the tree, using her top as a makeshift basket to hold them all.

'I have to apologise!' she wailed. 'I have to make this right!'

'I'm going to call a village meeting,' Nathair declared. 'Will you second me for it?'

Val nodded while she continued loading herself down with fresh apples. Nathair walked away, examining the fist-sized stone which had caused so much trouble. Whoever had taken the emerald must have known its effects, they knew how to use it, and they would have known about the faint resentment that Val must have felt every time that she saw someone taking from her tree.

Someone from the village, then, Nathair reasoned. *Whoever stole this must know the people of Arden intimately enough to know precisely where to apply pressure to make them explode. They also knew how to use the stone, which means that either they have received the same training as me, or they've borrowed it before.*

Either way, the answers would be found in the library records and Nathair found themself drawn to dive back into the sheets of data, looking for that elusive thread to pull on to start finding suspects, but putting an end to the stream of bitterness and petty discontent *had* to be the priority, so instead, they made their way to the village hall.

The sun was low in the sky by the time they were in sight of the old building and the solar tiles forming its roof shone brilliantly in the golden sun. Unlike most of the rest of the village's buildings, rebuilt from the ruins of other abandoned structures, the village hall had remained in continuous use from the Victorian era as a school and church, through the years of tumult as a community centre to the seat of the village council. When the council took over the building, it was sympathetically brought into modernity, with new technology like the solar tiles and thermal store glass incorporated without changing the character of the structure.

The door was unlocked, of course, and Nathair made their way into the lobby where a terminal sat on a carved wooden desk, inviting village residents to use it. Nathair fished their screen out of their pocket and found the contact that Alston had given them. They tapped her name and waited for her to answer.

'Hello?' the voice on the other end was clipped, direct, and exactly what Nathair needed.

'Alderman Elith, my name is Nathair. Your cousin gave me your contact details. I'm the—'

'You're the librarian,' she finished for them. Not unkindly, but with the air of someone wanting the other person to just get to the point. *'How can I help you, Mx Nathair?'*

Nathair straightened their shoulders and tried not to let the irritation of being cut off show in their voice.

'I would like you to put your name to an emergency council session,' they said, and tapped the computer's holo-screen. 'I believe that somebody from the village has stolen a number of sins from the library and is using them without consent of the people of Arden.'

'I see. To what end?'

'I'm not sure, but you must have felt the changes in the people's attitudes lately. Fences raised between long-term neighbours, petty arguments turning violent.'

'Hmm, I confess that council meetings have become more fractious of late,' the alderman admitted. *'All right, what is it you want to propose?'*

'To find the stolen crystals and have peacekeepers investigate and deal with whoever has been stealing them. I'm at the town hall now; I can schedule a meeting if you're able to propose it.'

There was a pregnant pause on the other end of the line, as Alderman Elith appeared to consider their suggestion.

'Is this really a matter for the peacekeepers?' she asked. *'We do have a reputation to consider...'*

'I would need to check my records, Alderman, but I don't recall lending you an emerald of pride lately...'

'A little civic pride isn't a sin, Mx Nathair.'

'I have a collection of shining yellow gems which would say otherwise, alderman,' Nathair joked and immediately hoped they hadn't pushed her too far.

'All right, point made. Fine, book a meeting and I'll propose it, do you have a seconder?'

'I do.' Nathair held back a deep sigh of relief and tapped to confirm the council meeting.

'Then I'll see you there. I expect you already have a suspect in mind?'

'I will do, I am going back to the library now to check through my records.'

Elith grunted and ended the call, but on the screen, the council meeting was proposed and a few minutes later seconded by Val. In short order, the booking began to fill with aldermen from across the village and the reality sunk in that Nathair would have to have something to present to them. They jumped from the chair and half-ran back out onto the street and towards the library. The sun had truly begun to set, and Nathair was painfully aware of the seconds slipping away before they would have to speak in front of the entire council with their findings as the last of the golden rays slipped behind the trees.

As they walked, Nathair tried to pin down what they were so nervous about. After all, they had addressed the council plenty of times, they were used to speaking to people about their most intimate of worries and concerns and they certainly weren't afraid of the inevitable arguments.

But you've never accused anyone of theft before. The realisation settled in their stomach like a stone. They would be directly pointing the finger at somebody they knew. Perhaps by the end of the night they might even have a name, they could be in the room, directly in front of them, protesting their innocence and accusing Nathair of stirring trouble, demanding to see evidence…

Nathair shook their head, such worries weren't helpful, focus on the now, on what could be done, and that was something Nathair was far more comfortable with – reviewing records.

The streetlights began to glow a soft, pale bioluminescent blue-green as Nathair crossed the narrow roads towards the library where the rainbow-glow of a thousand crystals provided more light through the windows than the streetlights possibly could. Nathair frowned, they *knew* what the lights of the library looked like, knew every sparkle and reflection through the glass, and tonight there was something *wrong* about how the light played over the brickwork walls. Nathair felt the hairs on the back of their neck stand to attention and they slowed to examine the structure more closely.

AN EMPIRE OF PAPER

There. A window on the west side, looking out over a badly maintained vegetable patch and a dwarf wall separating it from the road, instead of the regular play of light across the pane, it glistened and glimmered where the surface was broken and shattered. Nathair's eyes followed the multicoloured sparks shining in the weeds which had been trampled down flat.

Nathair felt their breath catch in their throat as they hurried to unlock the front door. Their shaking fingers stumbled over the keys in their pocket, and the little metal object slipped out of their clammy grip. Eventually, they were able to steady themselves enough to unlock the door and get inside, where the true extent of the damage became obvious. Shards of glass lay strewn over the floor, reflecting the glow of the emeralds like a kaleidoscope onto the shelves and ceiling in a line from the broken window, past the lines of emeralds and towards the desk at the centre of the room.

'No,' Nathair choked aloud. The book containing their handwritten duplicates lay open on the wooden surface and from even so far away, they could see that pages had been torn brutally from its spine. Scraps of paper littered the desk like giblets from a prey animal eviscerated by predators. They stumbled to the desk and switched on the holo-screen, knowing at least the electronic records were safe. That was until the screen fired up and garbled nonsense greeted Nathair. No matter where they clicked or scrolled, the screen could offer up nothing but scrambled letters and half-formed entries. 'No, no, no, no, no!'

Nathair collapsed into their chair, feeling like a part of themself had been torn from them. They glanced around the room; suddenly they couldn't remember whether the gaps staring back at them were new or whether they had been there from before. Had somebody moved around the positions of some of the stones? If the library had been a reassuringly calm lake, it now churned with uncertainty and doubt, leaving Nathair flailing in the middle of it, thrashing for any piece of flotsam to stay afloat. Nathair stood on unsteady feet and walked towards the door, intending to lock it, until the futility of that struck them and they walked instead to the calming blues of the emeralds of Sloth. They found a well-handled midnight blue stone of Deep Sleep and took it back with them to the chair. After a few seconds of staring, their eyelids drooped heavily, and they fell into unconsciousness.

~

One benefit of the Deep Sleep emerald was that the user was untroubled by dreams and disturbances, they would simply drift away into a sleep as deep as the blue of the crystal and awaken when they mentally reminded themself to. The downside to the Deep Sleep emerald was that the user would be untroubled by *any* disturbance, so Nathair awoke groggily to find themself in the middle of a crowd of deeply worried neighbours shaking their shoulder and calling at them to wake up.

"It's all right, Phyllis! They're awake!'

Nathair rubbed the sleep from their eyes and took the second or two needed to focus their vision on the figure standing over them. Resplendent in a tailored cream suit complete with a top hat adorned in a peach bow to match the tie and cummerbund. Once Nathair came to their senses, they realised that they weren't alone, but the library was filled with people in elaborate formal dress, from long flowing gowns to bejewelled tunics.

'Am I getting married?' they slurred.

'No, but I am!'

'Ah! Alston, I'm so sorry, I…'

'Alston-Gray now, thank you!' He said, grabbing a man in a near-identical suit. 'We were walking from the village hall to Cox's place for dinner—'

'—and concerned about why our favourite librarian hadn't shown up—'

'—even if they booked a council meeting on the day of our wedding—'

'—when we noticed the broken window. What happened?'

They explained everything to the gathered crowds, from the stolen gems, how they were being used to manipulate the people of Arden, the break-in and theft of the library records. When somebody suggested calling the peacekeepers, Nathair could only smile wanly.

'What would be the use? If they wanted to look for fingerprints, they would have hundreds of suspects,' they said, looking at the well-dressed crowd leaning against the shelves, or drumming their fingers on the corner of the desk. 'I'm guessing that you all have little shards of glass in your shoes, and I don't suppose people kept out of the gardens?'

There were a series of awkward glances and shuffling as people subtly tried to wide the traces of mud off their shoes.

'We don't need fingerprints or boot-prints,' said a voice from the back of the crowd, which parted at the insistence of Val's sharpened elbows. 'You just need to know who had a motive. Whoever has been stealing your crystals has been doing so for months, why would they break in last night?'

The fog of the Deep Sleep lifted like the sun itself had emerged to burn it away.

'Because they knew that I was going to expose them at the council meeting,' Nathair gasped. 'But I hadn't put that in the meeting proposal. The only people who knew were you and…'

Their eyes scoured the crowd until they settled on a woman edging through the crowd towards the door in a dark suit and trying to keep her head down.

'Alderman Elith!'

The crowd gasped and opened up a circle around the alderman, leaving her exposed and alone. To her credit, she straightened herself and smoothed out her suit, trying to portray herself as having deliberately chosen to stand out.

'I don't understand, why would you of all people…'

'I meant what I said on the screen last night,' she said. 'Civic pride isn't a sin, and yet here you have it bottled up, labelled, controlled alongside righteous fury, jealous passion, even something as simple as choosing to prioritise your own sleep. We managed to get through the years of tumult without needing to have everything that makes us human neatly wrapped up and filed away on a shelf somewhere.'

She dominated the space, turning the library into her own soapbox and the wedding crowd into supplicants ready to hear her words.

'I didn't *steal* the sins from this place, I liberated them. Gave them back to the people of Arden to live with, so that they could learn to control themselves, rather than having what makes them human controlled by glowing rocks overseen by an unelected tyrant,' she declared. 'We'll close the library, repurpose it into something we actually *need* instead.'

To Nathair's surprise, there were murmurs in the crowds, whispers and discussions seriously considering Elith's proposal.

'Is that really what you think that this place does? Control people?' Nathair retorted, speaking over the mutterings of agreement. '*People* control their emotions; no psyche emerald in the world is going to stop someone from being greedy or wrathful. The libraries are simply stores, somewhere people can put those emotions when they're not productive and pick them up and use them again when they need them.

'There's no charge here, no "tyrant" deciding who can have access to what, unlike you.'

'*Me?*' Elith protested. 'In case you hadn't noticed, *I* was elected by the people of this village.'

'Really? Val, did you elect to overreact to the neighbourhood children taking apples from your tree? Phyllis, did you give the alderman here permission to make you greedy and bitter about your relationship? How many more sins did you force people to experience without their consent for the sake of your beliefs?'

The murmuring had turned angry and Elith backed away from the frowns and sharp expressions on the faces of her neighbours.

'What's the matter, alderman? I thought that you believed people wouldn't experience wrath because the library controls it all?' They gestured to the shelves of red crystals lining the shelves on the far end of the library. 'There are the wrath emeralds, so where is this coming from?'

'I don't know how you're doing it, but you're controlling

them!' Elith snapped.

'How? Until the lovely Alston-Gray arrived, I was fast asleep,' they reasoned. 'The library isn't about control, but it *is* about power. It gives people the power to use these otherwise dangerous emotions in helpful ways, it gives people somewhere to come to understand them, and it takes power away from those who would exploit and provoke them as demagogues did in the days of the tumult.'

Elith tried to draw herself up, to rebut Nathair's arguments, but even she could tell that the tide of the crowd had moved against her. Reluctantly, she set her jaw and marched towards the door, feeling the weight of jeers and judging eyes on her back.

'This isn't over,' she spat as she reached the door.

'No, it isn't,' Nathair agreed with her, solemnly. Then smiled. 'You have, by my count, twenty-four emeralds scattered somewhere around the village. I'll have them back by the end of the day, or the peacekeepers can retrieve them from you.'

Elith scowled, then stormed out of the library, to cheers from the assembled partygoers.

'Now,' Nathair said, clapping their hands together. 'I

hear that the next stop was Cox's for food? If people want to get the most out of it, the gluttony emeralds are the orange stones on that shelf there…'

ABOUT THE AUTHOR

Christopher P. Garghan was born and raised in Birmingham and the city of a thousand trades winds itself into his every story, no matter the genre.

He currently has stories published in Optopia, a Solarpunk Zine; City of Night, City of Hope, and City of Echoes, three anthologies of short stories published by Birmingham Writers Group. and The Mapmaker Moths was his first self-published collection of short stories.

An Empire of Paper represents a selection of his writing over the last five years.